WELCOME TO HIGH SCHOOL, CHRISTOPHER THOMAS

~Freshman Year at Wilson High~

CHRIS MERANTE

JMJ PUBLISHING
NEW YORK

Welcome to High School,
Christopher Thomas
Copyright © 2017 by Chris Merante
All rights reserved.
Published by JMJ Publishing

Library of Congress Cataloguing-in-Publication Data
Merante, Chris, 1974-
Welcome to High School, Christopher Thomas-Freshman Year
at Wilson High / Chris Merante

Cover Photo by Josef Hanus–Courtesy of ShutterStock
JMJ Publishing Logo by Svetlana Corghencea–
Courtesy of 123RF

ISBN-10: 0692802606
ISBN-13: 978-0692802601
1. High School 2. Adolescence 3. The 1950's
4. Rock 'N' Roll Music 5. Pop Culture

First Edition

1 2 3 4 5 6 7 8 9 10

Printed in the United States of America

This book is dedicated to my loving wife, my four beautiful children, and my supportive family. You have inspired every page. I have been blessed.

CONTENTS

~ ONE ~

"There is nothing to fear but fear itself."
FRANKLIN DELANO ROOSEVELT

It was the twenty-ninth of August 1958, and our gang was looking for one more burst of excitement and adventure before the summer officially came to a close. Five of us teenage boys gathered around the tallest tree at the top of Bailey Hill. Evening began to give way to the night. Our silhouettes emerged in front of the deep-red sun that painted the sky orange just moments before it sank below the horizon. Nestled up in the tree was a muscular kid with a red handkerchief wrapped around his forehead. He inched out on his stomach to the edge of the longest branch. It must have been at least thirty feet off the ground.

"All right, sports fans, are you ready for this? This is the coolest thing I've ever come up with," Nick said. He finished tying a solid knot in a long piece of rope that descended from the branch to the onlookers below. "Wow! You can see the whole town from up here. You guys gotta come up!"

"No thanks. Some of us are anxiously waiting for you to come back down!" Goodie said. Sebastian "Goodie" Goodsen was going to be a freshman at Wilson High, along with Nick and me, when school started.

"Once I secure this rope, I'll climb down, okay? Don't worry. This is gonna be a lot of fun. I promise!" As Nick Armstrong maneuvered his way down the tree, one could not help but admire his athletic physique. His quarterback arm was lean. The sun glistened off of the crucifix that hung around his neck. The girls loved him. Why wouldn't they? His sleeveless shirts showed off his bulging biceps. The only thing more impressive than his muscles was his huge smile.

"So whose name does he have 'tattooed' on his arm this week?" I asked.

"It's Sandy this week. Pretty cute girl, huh? Of course, you know that's subject to change within five days," Charles said. My brother, Charles, was going to be a junior. He was the oldest in our

1

group who led by example. Everybody in the neighborhood looked up to him, especially me.

"I don't know, gentlemen. I don't have a good feeling about this. I don't think we should let him go through with it."

"Don't worry, Goodie. Never doubt the amazing Nick," I said. "I've seen this guy come up with more inventions in the past ten years than Thomas Edison did in his whole lifetime. Remember the time he made a rocket out of firecrackers and that old metal pipe he found in the garage? You could give Nick a paper clip, a rubber band, and a wooden spoon and not only could he make it fly, but he'd send it soaring from here straight to Tipperary Hill." Goodie smiled.

The last member of the group, who could no longer be silent, stood with a skeptical look on his face and a pack of cigarettes rolled up in his shirt sleeve—a kid we simply referred to as "Porter." Porter was an enigma. We were not even sure if he was going to be a junior or a senior. He had enough credits to be somewhere in-between. His favorite T-shirt read, "What are you lookin' at?" A noticeable gap between his two front teeth made it easy for him to spit on little Goodie when he felt the urge. There was a rumor floating around that he always wore blue jeans to cover up a scar his old man gave him on his right leg. Last year he was suspended from school for climbing the flagpole during the pledge of allegiance. Do you know why he did it? He did it because Nick bet him five bucks that he was too chicken to try, that's why.

"This is a huge waste of time. He doesn't really think that rope will hold, does he? It'll snap in two like a toothpick," Porter said.

"That's it, sports fans! It's all set. Look out guys. I'm gonna be the first to test this baby out!"

"Okay, Nick. Now enlighten us as to why we're up here. What are you gonna do with this thing?" Charles asked.

"Let me explain my wonderful new invention that will give us hours of enjoyment. Once you take a ride on this, every girl in New York will wanna go with ya to the Homecoming Dance. That is...if you're man enough to try it. I present to you 'Nick's Great Adventure Ride.'"

"Quit screwin' around and get to the point," Porter said.

"You will notice that this is one of the heaviest ropes in all of Onondaga County. You will also notice I have secured the rope to the end of the longest branch of the tallest tree on Bailey Hill. It's approximately thirty feet above ground level where we currently stand. If you take a peek over the edge of the cliff you'll see a frightening drop of another thirty feet down to those apple trees below."

I pulled my brother off to the side. "Charles, ya really think I could get a date to the Homecoming Dance by doin' this?" I asked. He laughed without giving a reply. I looked out over the town. It was a long way down all right.

"Now, I measured the rope so that it's long enough to allow someone to grab it and swing out over the apple orchard below and return safely to the bottom of the tree right here."

"You're nuts!" Porter said.

"You're not really gonna…"

"No, Goodie…*I'm* not gonna, but *we* are."

"No way! That's suicide!" Charles said.

"I'm not gonna try that. What if your hands slip off?" I said.

"Are you kiddin'? You're tellin' me you're not strong enough to just hold onto a rope? C'mon guys, don't be wimps. It'll be great!"

"Gee, Nick. I don't think this is such a good idea," Charles said.

Then our sister, Mary, showed up. She was going to be a sophomore. All the guys at school flipped for her petite, athletic body. She was one of the popular cheerleaders. Mary's trademark ponytail and pink warm-up outfit turned every guy's head. She always acted like she was the coolest member of the Thomas family.

"Charles? Chris? Mom sent me up here to tell ya dinner is gonna be ready in ten minutes? Ya need to get home. Now!"

"Hey, Mary! Ya wanna see my new invention?"

"Never mind her, Nick. Just show us how this thing works if you're so confident in it," Charles said.

"That rope isn't strong enough," Porter said.

"Sure it is. I bet my life on it."

"Then why don't you go first?"

"Okay, I will. Everybody back up."

Nick took the red handkerchief off of his forehead and threw it to the ground. He reached up, grabbed the rope, and tied it around his arms. His hands squeezed it as hard as they possibly could. A bead of sweat ran down the side of his face. He took a deep breath and then ran as fast as he could toward the edge of the cliff. I did not know if I should marvel at his bravery or laugh at his stupidity.

"He's really gonna do it!" Goodie said.

"Nick, wait! Stop! C'mon guys, let's grab him!" Charles said. Goodie and I joined in the chase. Nick picked up speed. As we closed in on him, Charles reached, grabbing only air. I lost my footing and slid out of control toward the edge. The adrenaline in my body surged as Charles pulled me back.

"Are you okay, Chris?"

"Yeah, I'm fine."

We were so caught up in the moment we forgot why we were running in the first place. Suddenly we heard a loud cheer.

"Woooooohooooo! Yeah! This is the greatest creation ever!" Nick shouted as he swung out over the orchard below. He did it! We watched as he swung toward us and jumped back onto safe ground.

"You boys are crazy and you're all gonna get hurt if you don't stop foolin' around. You two better be home in five minutes. I'm gettin' outta here," Mary said.

"Ya didn't think it would work, did ya, Porter?"

"Big deal!"

"Oh, yeah? If it's no big deal, why don't you try it?"

We all froze. When you are young, dumb, and most importantly, a male teenager, you can never turn down a challenge and show your face in town again. Porter never backed down from anyone.

"Ya think I'm scared?"

"No, I don't *think* you're scared, Porter. I *know* you're scared."

"You know what I think of your ride? Nothin'. That's what I think of it. That don't scare me in the least."

"Okay, then try it, big shot!"

Without another word, Porter grabbed a hold of the rope without a single expression on his face and bolted toward the cliff. It happened so quickly Charles did not even have a chance to talk him out of it. Porter flew out over the orchard. Without making a sound, he stared at the houses and streets in the distance. When he came back to safety, he immediately ran over to Nick.

"Is that proof enough for ya? Ya know what I think of your 'ride' now...nothin'."

"You're crazy, Porter. You risked your life just to prove a point?" Goodie said.

"Okay guys, now you've both proven you're tough. Let's call it a day. I don't think anybody else is crazy enough to try this thing," Charles said.

"Yeah, let's get home for dinner, Charles," I said.

"Hold on a minute. I'm not finished with Porter yet," Nick demanded.

With all his athletic might, Nick threw Porter over his shoulder, grabbed the rope, and instead of tying it around Porter's arms, he tied it around his ankles. As Nick took him off his shoulder we all watched as Porter dangled there upside down.

"There you go, tough guy. Does this scare ya?"

"Nothin', Nick. Nothin'."

We all begged them to forget this whole thing, but they simply would not quit. We all assumed Nick was just trying to scare Porter. We did not think he would actually push him out over the edge while he was dangling there upside down. It suddenly became a reality. Using his physical prowess to his advantage, Nick held onto Porter and took off running. He ran faster and faster.

"How 'bout now?"

"Nothin'!"

Goodie, Charles, and I held our breath. With one last rush of energy, Nick fired Porter out over the edge of the cliff, headfirst. We tried, but failed, to grab him as he swung back toward us.

"How 'bout now, wise guy?"

Porter laughed out loud. His face passed by us, upside down, and he said, "Nothin'."

While ignoring Charles's pleas, Nick gave Porter another push. We watched as his body flew out over the village again. This time, as the rope extended to its full capacity, we suddenly heard a dreadful sound. The rope broke just like Porter said it would. His body was launched like a missile. We watched in disbelief as he soared across the sky. In what seemed like slow-motion, the human rocket ripped through the humid air. He barely cleared the rock-filled creek below and landed in an apple tree. Birds spit out in all directions. We all raced down the hill.

"You see, you idiot! I told you to drop it before someone got hurt!" Charles scolded Nick.

"Oh, my God! I'm so sorry. I didn't think it would break. I hope he's okay."

Porter was wedged between two large branches. His body was contorted like one of those circus performers. Goodie feverishly climbed up into the tree to free him. "I got him! Grab him as I pry him loose." We took Porter by the arms and legs and slowly lowered him to the ground.

"Porter, Porter, you okay?" Charles pleaded.

"Porter, talk to us, buddy!" I said. I will never forget what happened next as long as I live. With an arm twisted and bruised, and a leg pointed at a ninety degree angle, Porter lifted his head, looked at Nick with a toothless smile and said, "Nothin'."

~ TWO ~

"An eye for an eye, and soon the whole world is blind."
                                    MOHANDAS GANDHI

It all started back in grade school. Growing up a short, chubby kid made me an easy target for the bullies. I would not have made it through those years if not for people like my friend, Goodie. We began eating lunch together in fifth grade when a couple of kids picked on the two of us late bloomers. Goodie convinced me there was strength in numbers. We had been buddies for a while, but that stressful year sealed our friendship for a lifetime.

I caught a few breaks as I entered adolescence, but lack of confidence plagued me. With my recent growth spurt, I shot up ten inches in nine months. I shed my baby fat and developed muscles, which I stared at for hours in the mirror. However, my future in high school was still unknown. I was going to be a freshman and I had no idea what to expect. Would I be able to make friends? How could I make a name for myself? What would the girls think of me? Would I become a jock? A nerd? A musician? An actor? A rebel?

The only thing I did know was that I had to get a pretty girl to go with me to the Homecoming Dance. If I did not get a date to the dance, people would label me a loser for the rest of my years in high school. I could not let that happen. I knew I needed help. My brother, Charles, guided me along. He was my mentor.

Charles and I had similar views and similar tastes. He tried to convince me we would be the coolest guys in school. I was not buying it. That little, pudgy kid that got picked on was always inside me.

We created a game plan for how I would secure a date for the big night. Before freshman year began, I adopted Charles's style as my own. I wore whatever he told me to and I wore it the way he told me to. We dressed almost identically except for different colors. We looked polished and cool, but also kind of tough. It was a whole new me.

Charles was a good-looking kid. He had one cool lock of hair that fell forward. I tried to do the same with mine, but it was never quite like his. Every summer my hair turned blond at the ends. One time this girl at school told me how nicely it complimented my blue eyes. I thought she was just teasing me though.

The summer had officially come to an end. Porter escaped from his "skydiving" impression with a whole lot of scrapes and bruises, some dental repairs, and a badly injured arm. Aside from the "adventure ride gone wrong" we had a lot of fun that summer. Hours of basketball, swimming, and playing "ghosts in the graveyard" were over for another year. I looked forward to the following summer when I planned on hitting on some girls with Nick and Charles instead of just watching all the action from the sidelines. I hoped the gang would still be together to pick up where we left off, but a year is a long time.

When Labor Day hit, the butterflies of going back to school started flying around in my stomach. It was worse than ever. There is nothing in the world that makes me angrier than the sound of my mother waking me up in the morning for the first day of school. I love her very much and I am sure I will look back on it fondly someday, but when she starts in with her personal version of "Reveille" every muscle in my body tenses up. "Chriiiiiis, time to get up, time to get up, time to get up in the mooorniiin'!" I want to slap her silly.

My first day of high school started out just as I feared it would. The initial incident occurred with this ridiculous freshman folder. I received it in the mail a few days before school started. It contained my schedule of classes and a map of the building. I hid it in my bag to conceal its awful, yellow color. If people spotted it, they would know I was a freshman right away—how embarrassing.

I got off the bus and entered the school half-jittery and half-asleep. Charles and Mary pointed me in the right direction and then they were on their way. Stupid me, I got lost within the first five minutes of being in the building. I did not want to have to pull out the folder, but I needed the map to figure out where my first class was.

As I reached into my bag, someone bumped into me from behind. All my papers went flying. As I frantically tried to gather them up, some lady stopped to help. I stood up and saw a friendly face say, "Here you go. Do you need help finding your way?" She was kind of short and very happy for some reason. I could not possibly imagine why, especially on the first day of school. I found out later that her first name was Joy. I got a kick out of that.

"I'm tryin' to find Room 210. Could you please tell me where it is?"

"Sure. Go down to the end of this hall and take a right. It's the third door on your left. I'm Ms. Button, the drama teacher...and you are?"

"My name's Christopher Thomas. Pleased to meet you," I said as we shook hands.

"Thomas, huh? Why does that name sound familiar? Are you signed up for one of my classes?"

"Uh...let me look at my schedule. I have...uh...'Introduction to Drama' last period. Let me see...it says the teacher is...Button. I guess that's you, right?"

"Yep. Well, I'll see you last period. Welcome to high school, Christopher Thomas. I hope you make the most of it."

"Thank you for your help, Ms. Button. I'll see you later," I said. Then she threw me this huge smile and walked away. The day slowly got better from that point on, but I was relieved when it was over.

As we cleared the hurdle of the first week of school, we all met, as usual, at Yorkie's Place around three o'clock. Yorkie was a funny, old Polish man who owned the joint. Everyone called him Yorkie because he was the biggest New York Yankee fan who ever lived. His diehard devotion was unparalleled. It ate him up inside when the Yanks lost a game.

Porter loved to show up wearing his Red Sox hat. Yorkie often tried to rip it off his head, but seldom succeeded. One time Mickey Mantle went hitless through three straight games. Porter started calling him Mickey "I have no dickey" Mantle. Yorkie got so mad he ran around the counter and chased Porter right out the door. It was hilarious.

This one day in particular, I was entertaining the guys with some impressions when all the trouble began. I started doing impressions for my family when I was very young. I loved stepping outside of myself and pretending to be someone else. As I got older, I shared them with the guys. Our science teacher, Mr. Bulbsey, was one of my favorites. His high, pinched, nasal voice was quite a challenge. I studied his gestures and favorite sayings all day so I could perform them at Yorkie's for the gang.

I pulled my pants way up over my belly button, tucked my head down, lowered my eyebrows in the middle, and pressed my lips together. "Listen Mister, I'm the teacher in this science class. Not you. You just shut up, Porter!" Bulbsey always told Porter to shut up, completely at random. "Today I'm gonna explain how you all can become the lady-catcher I am by makin' a few slight alterations to your physical being. First, I must tell you to repeat after me. *Shine + dine + whine = fine.*" They repeated in unison. "First, you need to *shine*. I mean that literally. Every morning when you wake, apply at least a half a pound of lard to your hair. This will give it a manly shine that exudes masculinity, not unlike Superman himself. You'll be able to slide a comb through it with great ease. This creates my customized rolling hill and valley look.

"Simply apply a piece of tape to the very center of your glasses to hold 'em together. This also helps reflect light and comes in handy as a safety feature when walkin' home after collectin' bugs at night. Golly Gee, don't laugh at me just 'cause I know how to utilize school supplies properly." Nick cackled as I wobbled around the room.

"Porter, shut up! Second, you need to *dine* correctly. My diet consists of mayonnaise, bacon, and ice cream. You don't have to eat all three together. But now that I mention it...that's not a bad idea." The guys exploded in laughter. "Gettin' back to the point at hand, one must start the day with fatty products in your hair and in your stomach. By eating these you will develop a very distinguished midsection. The women won't be able to stop staring, believe me...some children stare too, but you'll learn to ignore them. Once you reach this point, pull your belt up over your jelly belly so the buckle rests just below the nipples, like so." Goodie almost fell out of the booth as I demonstrated.

"Now it won't be easy to find too many pairs of pants that will conform to this unique shape. I'm able to get by on two pairs each year, the standard brown and black. One time my brown bombers were so comfortable I worked 'em over for a week straight. I even slept in 'em. Porter, you better shut up and I mean right now!

"Third, is the final component of this equation—the *whine*. Your woman has to whine, actually beg for mercy when you're with her in the evenings. That's right gentlemen; I'm talking about a three-letter word...and it happens to be spelled...G...A...S. I've squeezed out a few dingers that have rolled our family beagle right over." Porter sprayed his milkshake out onto the floor.

"You see in order for your woman to truly respect you, she must know you can generate some wind strong enough to send Dorothy back to Kansas! It's the only way a woman will honestly respect her man. In fact, this element is so important that I'll be starting a workshop after school each day that focuses specifically on flatulence. I call it 'Root for a good Toot!'" Charles could barely catch his breath.

"We'll start with the aroma factor. You need somethin' potent enough to get your lady's attention, without actually offending yourself. Next, we'll practice sound frequencies. I'll show you techniques to help you create 'sneaky squeakies,' 'foghorn fannies,' 'sharp shooters,' and of course, my favorite, 'the three-gun salute," but that takes practice and a tremendous amount of sphincter control. I'll demonstrate walkin' away from the scene of a crime without gettin' blamed for disturbing the peace. And finally, we'll talk about what to do with soiled underwear. So gentlemen, if you follow my directions, I'll quickly turn you into a doctor of love. Just remember my motto, *'Shine + dine + whine makes you oh, so fine,'* thank you," I said and bowed to my audience. They ripped up into applause.

"Man, that's gold!" Charles said.

"Yeah, you get funnier with those impressions every time," Goodie said. Some of the other kids in the place had also gathered around for a few laughs. I felt ten feet tall. They all went back to their booths as I fixed my pants and combed my hair. It was a typical afternoon at Yorkie's. We loved hanging out there.

Yorkie had a nice place. A long countertop in front of the kitchen formed a large semicircle. Little clusters of ketchup, mustard, and napkins lined the counter. The older people sat up there while they drank coffee and read the paper. Sometimes the "misfits" from school hung out there too just looking for trouble. The stools were shiny silver with round, red vinyl covers. They looked like candy. The black and white, square tiles of the floor reminded me of a chessboard. However, nothing compared to the booths.

The booths were our own private offices. Yorkie hung a poster above each one. They were comforting pages from our childhood scrapbooks. Charles and I started out at the booth with the Lone Ranger poster. We listened to his show on the radio every Sunday night. Our imaginations ran wild with the stories that emanated from that magical box by the fireplace. The Lone Ranger was every eight-year-old boy's hero. The day we heard we could go to the movie house and see him up on the big screen was like Christmas all over again. We cheered and laughed and shouted through the whole movie. The Lone Ranger was my first movie idol who I ironically got hooked on by listening to him on the radio.

Years later, we moved to Joe DiMaggio's booth. My father told us to cheer for him not only because he was a Yankee, but also because he was Italian. Charles and I were unbelievably proud of "Joltin' Joe's" fifty-six game hitting streak. We were convinced it would never be broken. We did a lot of bragging about his marriage to Marilyn Monroe too. Who wouldn't?

Once we made it to high school we sat at the booth in the corner with the poster of the original rebel himself—James Dean. Charles and I thought he was the coolest guy ever. Once we hit puberty, we started emulating the guys who got all the girls. In the movies, Dean went from Natalie Wood to Elizabeth Taylor, not bad. When *Rebel without a Cause* came out Dean wore a red jacket with blue jeans and a white T-shirt. All the girls went crazy for him—so all the guys went shoppin' for red jackets, blue jeans, and white T-shirts.

In the corner stood Yorkie's irreplaceable Wurlitzer jukebox. Every single day after school, kids filled the place and listened to the latest songs by Elvis Presley, Buddy Holly, Chuck Berry, Fats Domino, Little Richard—you name them, Yorkie had them.

The delightful aroma of grilled cheeseburgers and French fries stretched outside the front door and lured people into the place. Julia Romano, Yorkie's best waitress, brought us our malted milkshakes, burgers, and fries. She was cute and had quite an upbeat personality. We were always greeted with a smile. She worked so much it was hard to imagine her in anything but her uniform.

As Julia dropped off our food, the jukebox suddenly went silent. Everyone turned around to see Deke Marshall and his gang of thugs enter the room. They drove around town in his father's black '58 Dodge Royal, just looking for trouble. They always tried to pick fights with us. It had to be jealousy. Our crew had girls who talked to us, guys who admired us, and teachers, for the most part, who respected us.

Deke walked over to the counter and took a seat on a stool across from our booth. The rest of his followers sat down next to him. The five of them looked tough. I inched over closer to Charles. I put my hands in my pockets so no one could see them sweating.

"Look what we have here...a bunch of ladies sharin' a snack. Hey, look at the brothers. Notice how their mommy dresses 'em alike," Deke said. His boys moved in around us.

"Hey guys, did Old Man Henry's fertilizer truck just pull up? 'Cause it sure smells like crap in here all of a sudden," Nick said. We all laughed. Deke was not amused.

"Did you boys happen to get a look at that cheerleader this mornin'? Ya know, the blond with the pink outfit and the tight ass? I'm sure I'll be showin' her a good time at the dance next week," he said. Charles jumped up to defend our sister, but stopped himself before he did something he would regret. Nick and Porter stood up on either side of him.

"All right, Marshall. Just leave Mary out of this, okay? Do you really wanna bring sisters into this conversation? Because the last time I saw your sister she was so fat that when she farted she knocked a small kid off his bike."

I jumped in, "Hey, the last time I talked to her I said, 'What's shakin'?' and she answered, 'All four cheeks and a couple of chins!'" Goodie slapped my hand.

"Yeah, Marshall, next time we have a thunderstorm the five of us will just stand under her boobs to shield ourselves from the rain."

"Very funny, Porter. You're all hilarious. Well, we know we won't be seein' you losers at the Homecoming Dance 'cause they just announced it's gonna be a turnaround dance. That's right...this time the girls ask the guys. It looks like you wimps will all be sittin' home combin' each other's hair," he said, slapping his friend's hand in triumph.

"Deke, the only way you bums could find dates is if you go down to Warren Street and shell out five bucks apiece," I said.

"You wanna step outside, punk?"

"I'm not afraid of you!" I said, trying to keep my voice from trembling. Charles pushed me back down into the booth next to Goodie. Yorkie came out to see what all the commotion was. Charles held up a hand, letting him know he had the situation under control.

"Deke, why don't you just take a walk? We don't wanna fight in here. Just get lost," Charles said.

Nick and Porter looked away. They did not want to be pushed around by anyone. After some coaxing, Charles convinced them to back down. I exhaled a sigh of relief. Goodie's eyes calmed in agreement.

"Okay. We'll leave you chickens. Whenever you're men enough to take us on—we'll be ready. C'mon guys, let's split," Deke said. Then he snapped his fingers and they all left.

Nick grabbed Charles by the shoulder. "Why wouldn't you let us teach those boys a lesson?" he asked.

"You know that's not the way. We don't have to prove anything to them," Charles answered.

"This whole town will think we're chicken," Porter said.

"This whole town will think we're smart. What good would it do to throw punches with those hoodlums? We'd only look as trashy as they do. Besides, you don't wanna cause a stir in front of poor Yorkie, do ya?"

"I'd like to take that toothpick Deke chews and stick it down his throat!"

"I know you would, little brother. We all would. Do ya have any idea what Dad would do if he found us fightin' with those jerks? He would ground us for a year. Don't worry. Someday they'll all get what's comin' to 'em." Everyone went back to eating their meals. Yorkie turned the music back on and returned to his kitchen. Deke Marshall and his gang would not be causing anymore trouble that day.

THREE

"A teacher affects eternity; he can never tell when his influence stops."

HENRY ADAMS

As we finished off our milkshakes we all sat in silence for a few minutes, trying to forget about Deke Marshall. Charles's wheels were turning. Then he started in on Nick's favorite subject. "Hey, Nick, did ya happen to see Ms. Matheson today?"

"Of course I did! Isn't she the prettiest teacher you've ever seen? I think she's even one up on that Ms. Turner from the bank. I'm tellin' ya, Matheson dethroned her this year on the first day of school with that black outfit she had on."

"Did ya catch her erasin' the board yesterday after class?" Porter asked. "The way that body sways back and forth is poetry-in-motion."

"Gentlemen, I can honestly say she's certainly a beautiful woman. I'll give her that much," Goodie added.

"Well, have I got a story for you guys," Charles said. "Yesterday after lunch, Ms. Matheson was walkin' down the hall in front of me. I wanted to catch up to her to make small talk, ya know, anything just to talk to her. Nobody else was around; I coulda caught up to her, no problem. So I broke into a quick jog. Just as I got movin', she dropped a bunch of papers on the floor. At the precise moment I came up behind her, she suddenly stopped walkin' and bent over to pick 'em up. I slammed on the brakes, but it was too late. I slid and banged into her from behind."

"Are you kiddin' me? My brother is a maniac!" I said.

"Hold on, it gets better! I wrapped my arms around her to keep her from fallin'. So picture this. She was in front of me facin' forward. I got my arms around her waist as she started to straighten up. We both went flyin' against the lockers and then fell to the ground. She wound up right on top of me, face to face."

"No way!" Goodie said.

"You're makin' that up, Charles!" Porter said.

"You're right. I am!" We all went silent for a moment until Charles's words sunk in. Then we exploded on him.

"I don't believe it!" Nick said. He collapsed onto the table.

"You son of a gun, you! I knew that was too good to be true!" I said. We all sat stunned by the amazing images he created. Charles had done it again; Deke Marshall was long gone from our minds.

"I'm sorry, Nick...you okay, man?"

"You're evil. You're pure evil. When I told you that dream I had about her, I thought you understood how much I loved that woman and then you pull a stunt like this. I think I just had a heart attack."

"What dream did you have?" Porter asked.

"He dreamed that in the middle of a lesson about pen and ink sketches she jumped up onto the table and asked him if she could be his nude model," Goodie said.

"Okay. Make fun of me. You'll all see, one day I'll win her over. In fact, I wouldn't even be surprised if we end up goin' to the Homecoming Dance together."

"Keep dreamin'. Did you guys hear what happened to Woodcock today?" Porter asked. "He was liftin' these really heavy boxes of books in his classroom. We were all kinda laughin', watchin' him struggle. A couple of class nerds asked him if he needed help, but he said they were not strong enough. So they backed off. We hoped he would get a hernia or somethin' just because he was bein' such a jerk. He told us to read the chapter about the Trojan War; ya know, the story about the soldiers hidin' in the wooden horse and all? Just when it got perfectly silent in the room, he squatted down and we heard this loud 'rrrrrip!'"

"You're kiddin', he ripped his pants?" Charles said.

"Split 'em right where 'the sun don't shine!' A second after we heard the rip he went, 'Oh Shit!' Then he put his hand over his ass like he crapped his pants and ran outta the room!" We all laughed.

"That's incredible!" Nick said.

"He got what he deserved, that pompous jerk," Goodie added.

"I don't know what you're all laughin' at. He did what any good teacher would do in an uncomfortable situation. He used inappropriate language and then left the students unattended in the room," I said. They laughed at my deadpan expression.

16

Woodcock thought he was the coolest guy in town. One of our favorite games was seeing how many times we could walk by his classroom and yell "Woodcock!" without getting caught by him. Porter holds the record at thirteen in one day.

"None of you guys are takin' drama, right?" I asked. "Well, I actually have this really cool teacher. Her name is Ms. Button. She's great. You may have seen her in the hall; she's really short and full of energy. She put us into groups and made us improvise these different situations. It was a lot of fun. I think she likes me 'cause she chose me as her partner and we acted one out in front of the whole class. Who knows, maybe I'll get the lead in the play someday."

"Sounds like you got the hots for her," Porter said.

"No, it's not like that."

"A drama teacher? Aren't they kinda...different?" Nick asked.

"No, really she's great. I don't like her like I do Ms. Matheson, but I look up to her, ya know, like a mentor. She told me I should audition for the play. It's not like football, where the best man plays, in drama they always go with the older guys first. So I probably won't get a big part this year, but that's okay. I'll let Nick shine as starting quarterback. For now, I'd be happy with a small part. Maybe I'll make a name for myself down the road."

"I think that's great, Chris! You definitely have the talent," Goodie said.

"I don't know. I mean, your impressions and stories are great and all, but aren't you worried you'll get labeled as bein'...ya know?" Nick paused.

"Girlie," Porter blurted out. The others chuckled. I immediately began to panic. If girls got the wrong idea about me I would never get a date. I searched for a way out. I was two seconds away from saying it was all a big joke. Suddenly Charles bailed me out.

"C'mon guys, my little brother here has got some talent just like James Dean. Dean was an actor and he was pretty cool, wasn't he?"

"I guess so," Nick said. Porter nodded in agreement.

"Believe me...when you see what I do...it's a lot like the stuff that gets you guys laughin' here at Yorkie's."

"Well, I think you should definitely go for it, Chris. I know you'll be a big hit!" Goodie said.

"You really don't care if people talk about ya?" Porter said.

"Hey, my little brother has never let other people stop him before. Chris, if you think you can do it, then you should. Let us know when your auditions are. We'll come heckle you." That was all they needed to hear. I leaned back with ease. Charles really bailed me out of that one.

We spent the next few minutes arguing over the fries because Porter liked them with gravy, the old-fashioned way. We all thought ketchup was the cool thing to do. We settled for a little of both. By that time, we had covered science, art, social studies, and drama.

Nick took over, "I still think my favorite teacher is Mr. Leonardo, the math teacher. He's got a way about him that cracks me up. I can't explain it. Ya know how a lot of teachers either intimidate or become 'buddy buddy' with ya? Leonardo doesn't do that. He's nice, but sometimes he goes out of his way to tease us. Like the other day when Chris and I were in class, he wrote a two-part problem on the board. After he finished the first part, he started to walk to the other side of the board. He stopped in the middle, looked at us and said, 'Okay now I'm gonna walk to this side of the room to write part two, so why don't you make sure you forget everything I wrote over here in part one, okay?' I loved it. He's so damn funny."

"Yeah, I know. He's hilarious. We couldn't keep up with all his jokes that day. He makes algebra seem kinda fun," I said.

Charles decided to contribute once again, "You guys should see my history teacher, Mr. Conti. You talk about a character! He writes a ton of notes on the board, which is kind of a drag, but he makes me laugh. When the class gets talkin' too loud sometimes he stops writing on the chalkboard and he'll turn around and just stand there with this deadpan look on his face. Then completely out of left field he'll go, 'Shut up!' really loud. It's shocking, I'm tellin' ya. Some of the girls in front of the room nearly jump out of their seats. It's hilarious."

"Ya know who my favorite history teacher is, gentlemen? Mr. Dwyer. I've always admired him because he's so well-read. He knows all there is to know about history. He's a very eloquent speaker too. I love the way he gets excited about literature and he tells all those great stories in class about when he was growing up and all the funny things his family did and everything, and ya know, he's a sharp dresser. Sometimes I just sit there and think in my mind how much I admire him and how I'd love to be like him someday and..." Goodie stopped, realizing he was holding a one-man conversation.

"Hey, Goodie, ya know he's psychic, right?" Porter said.

"What? No he's not!"

"Sure he is. He reads minds," Nick added.

"I think I heard that somewhere too," Charles said.

"One day I was sittin' there thinkin', 'God, this class is so long. When is it ever gonna end?' At that very moment he looked at me and said, 'Ten after nine.' He's got powers, Goodie—strange powers," Porter said as he winked at me.

"D'ya think he can hear me when I think he's a cool dresser and all?" Goodie asked.

"You know it. That's why he always gives you those funny looks. He probably thinks you like him a little too much, if you catch my drift. The next time you go to class be sure you monitor those thoughts of yours. Remember...he's listenin'," Porter said. Goodie slid down into the booth in serious contemplation. We muffled our laughter.

"This has been great, sports fans, but I gotta go home and clean my room before dinner or my mom will ground me for a month," Nick said.

"Chris, you and I better get goin' too. Mom asked me to get some milk and bread on the way home."

"I guess I'll get lost for a few hours," Porter said.

"Goodie, you leavin'?" I asked, shaking him out of his reverie.

"Huh? Oh, yeah...I have to get home and mow the lawn." He stood up and threw on his baby-blue jacket. We shouted a few good byes to fellow classmates on our way out. Of course, we had to pull Porter away from Yorkie because he was chanting, "Mickey, Mickey got no Dickey!"

FOUR

"Mid pleasures and palaces, though we may roam, be it ever so humble, there's no place like home."

JOHN HOWARD PAYNE

No matter what is going on in my life, my spirits are always lifted by my Mom's famous spaghetti and meatballs. If my friends hear she is making sauce, they always find a way to stop by at dinnertime in the hopes of getting an invitation. My parents were always accommodating.

My mother is one of the nicest people I know. Friends and neighbors always go out of their way to say hello to her. Her maiden name was Patricia Kelly. Her father was from Ireland, but her mother was straight from Italy and shared all her cooking secrets. Mom's hair was starting to gray and her face was getting round and more Irish-looking every day. Not only was she a great cook, but she was "the glue of the family."

If you caught my father on a good day, he could go on for hours and hours, telling stories and jokes. He was a fun person to be around, but he worried a lot. He grew up fast after his father died unexpectedly. Grandpa Thomas ran his own coffee business. Unfortunately, along with success came stress and worry that ultimately ended his life too soon. Being the oldest child, my father had to provide for his mother and seven younger siblings only a couple years after graduating from high school. Talk about pressure.

Charles thought Dad felt cheated and bitter about having to deal with too much responsibility at such a young age. I did not feel sorry for him, though. Not only did he take a pretty girl to the Homecoming Dance, but he was voted "Most Popular Boy" his senior year. I saw it right in his old yearbook. How can you argue with that?

People call him Jerry. His name was Jerome Tomasella. It's Italian, but my grandfather changed it to Thomas when he came to America. He got kicked around a lot by people who hated Italians. Back then, there were lots of people who hated Italians, lots who hated the Irish, lots who hated the Hispanics, and so on.

Your ethnicity determined where you lived, who you associated with, and even what job you had. My father constantly reminded us about all his parents endured to inspire us to work hard at creating a future for ourselves. Whenever he launched into one of his sermons my sister, Mary, would role her eyes in dramatic fashion.

Mary was also a lot of fun when she wanted to be. She was right between Charles and me in age. We did not hang out with her all that much at school because we kind of belonged to different crowds. Charles did his own thing and I was a grade below Mary. Hanging out with your younger brother at school was just not cool.

My parents raised us in an environment where conversation was always valued. As we finished this one particular sensational meal, we sat and talked. My mother began clearing the table with my sister's help. Charles and I sat with Dad. We began asking him all those questions kids typically have. Dad had all the answers.

Mom surprised us with half-moon cookies from Harrison's Bakery. They were our favorite. A half-moon cookie is about the size of the palm of your hand. They are soft, cake-like, and covered with vanilla frosting on one half and chocolate frosting on the other half. Porter constantly reminded us that they were really quarter-moon cookies, but that is another story. We each poured ourselves a tall, cold glass of fresh milk and enjoyed each other's company for a while. Unlike some kids, I loved spending time with my family. Besides, it got my mind off of the Homecoming Dance for a little while.

"That's a party for your mouth isn't it, Charles?" I said. He loved when I used those kinds of expressions.

"That's about the greatest dessert in the world, partner," he said.

"Did you boys know that the Campbells down the street installed an underground bomb shelter yesterday?" Dad asked.

"No. Is that a waste of money or what?" I said.

"Well...you never know."

"What d'ya mean, Dad? Ya don't think we'll get hit with the bomb, do ya?" Charles asked.

"Maybe we will...maybe we won't."

"Get outta town! Really, Dad?" I said.

"No, no, no. I'm only teasin'. We don't have to worry about all that business with the Russians droppin' a bomb on us. Listen boys, we don't have to worry about a thing. We live in the strongest country in the world. President Eisenhower won't let anyone mess with us."

"Then why do we do those stupid drills at school where everybody dives under their desks? I mean, what good is a desk gonna do, anyway, if a bomb lands on my head?" I said. Charles loved that one.

"Don't let that get to you, Son. The Campbells and other families like them are wastin' their money."

I decided to change the subject. I read this article in the newspaper about UFO's so I thought I would mention it. "Hey Dad, I still wanna know what ya think about that UFO they spotted out west." Mary joined us at the table.

"UFO? What does that stand for?" she asked.

"Unidentified flying object," Charles answered.

"You guys are so weird. Who cares about UFO's?"

"You'll care if a light comes through your window one night and burns your pretty little face off!" I said. Charles put her in a headlock while I practiced some wrestling moves on her.

"Stop it! Leave me alone! Dad, tell 'em to stop."

"All right, now let her go, Charles. Chris, that's enough." She fell back into her chair. We loved goofing around with her because she could not "pretend" to be all mature. We still loved acting like kids from time to time. Mom entered the room and came to Mary's defense.

"What's goin' on in here? Are you botherin' your sister again?"

"Be careful woman or they'll come after you next," Dad said.

"I'm not afraid of these two. Remember boys, I used to change your diapers."

"Yeah! She got you guys good with that one!"

"Ya think that's funny, Mary? That's not funny. Ya know what's funny?" Charles said as he got up from his chair. I closed in on Mary from the other side. He put her in a bear-hug as I imitated a good old eye gouge. We were a great tag team.

When we finally let her go, Charles turned the tables on me and joined forces with Mary. They worked me over for about three or four minutes. We ordinarily were not this silly, but it was

22

the first Friday of the school year. We had lots of pent-up energy that needed to be expelled. We took turns slapping each other around for a few minutes like a Three Stooges routine.

"Okay, stop all that foolishness. It's time to settle down," Mom said.

"Did I tell you about my friend, Lana Lorenza?" Mary asked.

"What about her?"

"She bought a Hula Hoop yesterday. It's amazing!"

"I heard people talkin' 'bout those at school, but I didn't think ya could buy 'em around here yet," I said.

"She bought hers in New York City this past summer. They get everything before we do 'cause they're such a big city."

"What's a Hula Hoop?"

"Jerry, you know what a Hula Hoop is. It's those new toys the kids play with. They're round and made of plastic," Mom said.

"Oh, yeah. You mean those things that you put around your waist and try to move around and around until you make yourself sick?" Dad threw me a wink.

"Dad, they're cool! You can't make fun until you try it. Lana Lorenza can get that thing goin' for hours. Our cheerleading coach said all the girls should get 'em 'cause they'll help us work on our rhythm and balance."

"You wanna work on your rhythm and balance? Go check out that noisy Rock 'N' Roll music your brothers are always listenin' to," Dad said.

"Hey, that's not fair. There's nothin' wrong with Rock 'N' Roll music. We listen to it 'cause it's cool. We're 'hip.' Isn't that right, Chris?"

"That's right, Charles. We're as cool as all those cats on the big screen, ya know, Elvis Presley, James Dean, and Marlon Brando rolled into one."

"Look out dear, they're speaking in foreign tongues again," Dad said.

"You didn't let me finish my story," Mary said. "I heard there was this boy at school who set the record by makin' the Hula Hoop go around his waist three thousand times!"

"Ya know what that kid needs?" Dad asked.

"What?"

"A good, swift kick in the ass, that's what he needs!" Charles and I burst out laughing.

"Jerry, don't talk that way at the dinner table!"

"You wanna hear somethin' funny? Ya know how Lana Lorenza's father is kinda well...how should I say it...fat."

"Mary! You shouldn't make fun of the poor man just because he's heavy, right Jerry?"

"What're you askin' me for?" he said, pulling in his stomach.

"Well, he must've confused moving his hips with sucking in his stomach. After a few times around, his pants fell down right to his feet!"

"Mary, that's not nice!" Mom said. Just then the telephone rang. Mom got up as always to answer it. "You people are not being very good Christians today. You better say you're sorry to God in your prayers tonight," she said.

"Hey, Dad, d'ya think the Yankees are gonna win the World Series again this year?" I switched to sports talk.

"They'll win it like they always win it. The only team in town that could take a shot at 'em was those Brooklyn Dodgers, but now they're out in Los Angeles."

"I don't see why they had to leave; their fans are heart-broken. I couldn't imagine losin' the Yanks to the West Coast," Charles said.

"Boys! Your friend, Andrew, is on the phone!" Mom called out from the kitchen.

"I'll see what he wants," Charles said.

"That Jackie Robinson sure was somethin'," Dad said.

"That reminds me...d'ya think it's gonna work with the black and white players playin' together?" I asked.

"Why wouldn't it work?" Mary said. "They're just as good as the white players, aren't they?"

"Of course they are, but I was askin' Dad if he thought it would work. You don't know the kind of abuse some of the white fans and players used to give Robinson."

"That's a good point, Son. Like anything in life, it'll take some time. I think if other black players can hang in there and prove they're just as good as the whites then no one will be able to deny them. After all, Robinson proved it when he won the Series a few years ago. No one can argue with a World Championship."

24

"It doesn't make sense. Blacks and whites can play ball together, but they have to use separate bathrooms and drinking fountains. It's absurd," Mary said.

"Maybe someday your generation will figure this whole thing out. That bus boycott down in Alabama a few years back sure was a successful way of solvin' that problem without anyone gettin' hurt. My advice to you kids is to stay clear of all of it. I don't want any of you gettin' into any trouble." Suddenly, I noticed Mary had this evil little smile on her face.

"Hey, Chris, did anyone ask you to the Homecoming Dance yet?" I could not believe she put me on the spot like that. Everything stopped. My father seemed awfully interested in my answer too. I did not know how to approach it.

"Uh, not yet really, but Charles and I are workin' on it." I wiped the sweat off of my forehead. "What about you, Mary? Did you ask anyone?"

"Well, I was thinkin' of askin' several different guys. I'll probably take one of the football players. I'm not worried about it; especially since I'm gonna do the askin'."

"Oh, it's one of those dances where the girls ask the guys, huh?" Dad said, glancing at me out of the corner of his eye. "I'm sure it'll all work out, Son. Some nice girl will ask you to go. Boy, I remember when I was a senior in high school. I had a lot of fun at my Homecoming Dance," he said.

"We know the whole story, Dad. You took the *prettiest girl in school* and were voted the *most popular boy*. You've told it a thousand times," Mary said, rolling her eyes.

Charles called out from the kitchen, "Chris, Drew wants to know if we wanna play 'Funball' with him over at Jack's house tomorrow."

"Yeah, that'd be cool."

"Okay, I'll let him know."

"You think you're gonna get a date to the Homecoming Dance playin' 'Funball' and actin' like a little kid?" Ouch! That hurt. I shook it off, realizing it was just Mary being Mary.

"I think your brothers like to pretend they're Joe DiMaggio and Mickey Mantle when they hit that puny, little ball out of your uncle's backyard."

"You guys need to get a life."

"Oh, yeah? Well, you need another eye gouge!" I grabbed her again. She hit me with a sucker punch. Dad yelled out orders like a referee in a boxing match. Mom scolded us from the kitchen. Charles shouted that he could not hear Drew on the phone. It was a chorus of love.

FIVE

"We would often be sorry if our wishes were gratified."

AESOP

Charles and I woke up early on Saturday. After mowing the lawn, we set out for Jack's around eleven o'clock. Jack was one of our favorite cousins. He was born just two hours after Charles. We have been close as far back as I can remember. Jack has a tremendous sense of humor and all the girls loved his clean-cut image. "Best Dressed" is definitely going to him in the yearbook. His perfectly-combed hair was movie-star quality.

Jack was always the center of attention. He had a magnetism that drew others to him. People loved being around him, that is, until he got mad. Jack had a temper unlike anyone else on the planet. When he loses it, it is best to walk away quietly. His face gets all red and his nostrils flair like cannons. Sometimes we would stop playing a game for fifteen minutes while he worked it out of his system. He would throw things, break things, and swear up a storm. Regardless of how he expressed himself, my brother and I consistently went home feeling like we got our money's worth. Jack could put on one heck of a show.

I almost forgot to mention the best part. Jack is barely five feet, six inches tall. He looks small and harmless, but he has the energy and fury of a lion. He is ferocious and dangerous when his blood is up. Unfortunately, it was Jack's anger that severed ties with Goodie and Porter.

One day we were playing football and Goodie had been putting pretty rough defense on Jack the entire game. Jack's anger was slowing building. When it came down to the last play, Jack did something that only he could think up. Rather than score a touchdown to win the game, he threw the ball off of Goodie's face. His team was furious with him, but he did not even care. He got his revenge. Poor Goodie's glasses broke right in half.

All I remember was Jack shouting, "Hike," and then he dropped back and yelled, "Come and get it, you son of a bitch!" We can laugh in retrospect, but it was kind of sad to see Goodie fall face-first into the mud. Jack was big enough to apologize later on, but it still scarred Goodie enough to keep him away from Jack's playground for good. Who could blame him?

Porter will not ever go over to Jack's again because Jack officially banned him from his house indefinitely. Porter played baseball with us one time at Jack's house and after the game he took Jack's ball and pretended it disappeared. My brother and I know the way Porter is so we thought it was funny. Jack did not.

I remember Jack shouting, "Give me my ball, you knucklehead!"

Porter said, "Ball, what ball? I don't see any ball."

Every time Jack turned around, Porter bounced it off the driveway. When Jack heard it, he turned to catch a glimpse, but Porter hid it too fast. This went on for twenty minutes. Jack finally blew his stack and kicked Porter out of his yard. He was the only kid who had the guts to kick someone out of his yard and get away with it. If he booted you out, nobody wanted to stick up for you because they would also risk getting thrown out.

You see, Jack had a really cool yard. My uncle made a good amount of money and he bought things before anyone else in the neighborhood. They had the first television set, the first basketball hoop, the first nice car, and a backyard that was the closest thing to Yankee Stadium we had ever seen. Of course, Charles and I remained loyal to him because he was family. All that other cool stuff did not matter to us...much.

Drew was Jack's sidekick. "Drew" is actually a nickname for Andrew, which in the original Italian is Andrea. We teased him about having a girl's name, but it was actually a popular male name back in Italy. We met back in fourth grade. He came from a "traditional Italian, Catholic family" as my mother would say. Every time he passed by a church, he blessed himself. Drew's kindness and calm demeanor made him quite popular. I guarantee he will get voted "Nicest Guy" in the yearbook.

On this particular day, Jack's sister, Anna, and her friend, Elizabeth, answered the door. Anna has always been a real nice girl. She was on the cheerleading squad with Elizabeth and my sister, Mary. I liked how she never looked down on me for being younger.

Let me tell you a little bit about her friend, Elizabeth Allen. She was, in my humble opinion, one of the most beautiful girls in

28

Wilson High history. She dated a lot of guys, including that slime Deke Marshall, which made her either famous or infamous, depending on whom you asked. Charles thought she was crude and obnoxious. I thought he had her all wrong.

Elizabeth Allen was flashy and exciting. No one ever called her Beth or Liz, only Elizabeth. I used to think she was way out of my league, but my growth spurt gave me new confidence. I had one huge advantage over the other guys; I could see her whenever I wanted to because she hung out with my cousin, Anna.

She could be a little overconfident at times, but that was what I liked about her. When people gave her attitude, she gave it right back. I think she kind of viewed me as Mary's cute little brother, but she never treated me like dirt. All the other guys who flirted with her got straightened out or slapped, but never me. I gave her flowers all the time when I was a kid, even junky, old dandelions. She always smiled and thanked me.

I had been thinking about Elizabeth a lot when freshman year started. She always popped into my mind when I was up late at night. As if getting a date for the big dance was not stressful enough, once it was made into a turnaround, I did not know if I would even go at all. I heard that Elizabeth had recently broken up with that jerk, Deke Marshall. Maybe there was a possibility she would go with me. I knew it was a long shot. If she asked me to the dance, I would be set for the rest of high school. No one would ever question my ability with the ladies.

I have to say that I was not a huge fan of this turnaround dance stuff. I had absolutely no control over it. My mom told me that was what girls felt like every time there was any kind of dance. I guess she was right. I was glad I was a guy.

The more I thought about getting a date with Elizabeth, the more it made sense. She always kind of flirted with me and even complimented me from time to time. That was the coolest thing in the world. I got first-class treatment from a beautiful girl who was not nice to very many people. That fascinated me.

I decided to pay extra-close attention to her that day. I just wanted some signal that she might be interested. If I needed a date, I was gonna start at the top. I did not care what Charles thought. I had nothing to lose.

When we arrived, Anna and Elizabeth were doing each other's hair and make-up while practicing their cheers for the big football game.

"Hey guys! Come on in, Jack and Drew are outside gettin' ready for the big 'showdown' today," Anna said.

"Yeah, those poor guys don't even realize how bad we're gonna beat 'em," Charles said.

"We'll beat 'em like we always beat 'em. How're the cheers comin', ladies?" I asked.

"The usual, ya know. We've been doin' it for so many years now we don't need much practice like some of the other girls," Elizabeth said. Charles rolled his eyes.

"We know. You're a couple of professionals. We constantly hear all of the younger girls at school sayin' how much they look up to you two."

"That's sweet, thank you, Chris. Your brother is quite the charmer, Charles," Elizabeth said. I smiled shyly. Was that my first signal?

"Yeah, that's my little brother all right. Hey, Anna, before I forget, here's one of my mom's recipes she asked me to give to your mom."

"Thanks. I'll make sure she gets it. Oh, I almost forgot, did you see our new television set? Come into the family room and take a look. It's amazing!" Anna led Charles into the other room. I fantasized about this being a little plan the girls devised so Elizabeth could get me alone. Charles did not believe girls did those sorts of things, but we did them all the time so I knew girls did them too. It's a game. Elizabeth played it well. She was the prettiest thing I had ever seen. Her beautiful, beaming smile drove me crazy. Only Elizabeth's perfectly-athletic body could make a T-shirt and shorts completely stunning.

"So, did ya know there's a sock hop at school after the big Homecoming game?" she asked, coming closer. Back in the day, teachers did not want the kids marking up the gym floor with their shoes so everybody danced in their socks.

"Yeah, I heard about that...the Homecoming Dance...it should be fun." The sudden quiet of the room made me a little uneasy. I pushed up my sleeves a bit so she could get a good view of my new muscles.

"I hope they play some cool songs. I told Lana Lorenza, she's the head of the Committee, 'Make sure you get a band that can play some of the newer stuff we can dance to.' Ya know, like the ones they play on *American Bandstand*?"

"Yeah, that's a great show. The host, Dick Clark, is pretty cool. Did ya know he went to Syracuse University?" I played with the bottom of my T-shirt to give her a quick glimpse of my stomach—no more baby fat.

"He went to school at SU, huh? That's interesting. Well, I'm sure it'll be a great Homecoming game next Saturday. Hey, your friend, Nick Armstrong, is the new quarterback this year, right? He's cute."

"Yeah. That's right. He's quite the athlete. So are ya goin' to the Homecoming Dance after the game?" I wanted to get her mind off of my "cute" friend.

"I've been thinkin' about it. How 'bout you?" She took another step closer. I kept trying to forget about that self-conscious, little pudgy kid she used to smile at. I was not a little kid anymore. I was a young man and I wanted her to know it.

"Well, it's a turnaround dance, isn't that right?" I thought by saying that I would give her a perfect opening to ask me.

"Yeah. It's a turnaround this time. I haven't asked anybody yet. I'm not quite sure if I'll go." Not go? I was sinking fast. I had to keep pushing ahead—flattery, I needed to use more flattery.

"Are you kiddin'? You're the best dancer in the whole school. Nobody can jitterbug like you."

"Thanks. I bet you're pretty good too, aren't you? You look like you could swing a girl around the dance floor." She took my hands as if she wanted me to prove it to her. They were so soft and delicate. Charles must have sensed we were getting too close.

"Chris, get in here and take a look at this television. It's incredible!" he shouted.

"Be right there!" I could not stop staring into her eyes. "I guess...we should...go take a look, huh?"

"Yeah, we probably should." She dropped my hands and walked into the family room. I missed my chance. Who was I kidding? She was not going to ask me out and I could not have mustered up the guts to accept anyway. She wanted a "Deke Marshall." I was still just a little kid in her eyes.

31

"Wow! That's quite a television set!" I said as I entered the room.

"Isn't it great? It's even bigger than our last one! We begged my dad to buy it for months. Jack even cleaned his room every day for a month. My parents had to give in."

"Have you seen *American Bandstand*?" Charles asked.

"Chris and I were just talkin' about it! It's the best! They play all the latest songs."

"I've seen it a few times. Everybody at school talks about it," Anna said.

I jumped back into the conversation, "Our parents are always tryin' to limit our TV time. We get to choose two shows a night. It's usually a battle between Jack Benny, 'Uncle Miltie,' or my Dad's favorite, *The Honeymooners*. They're all pretty good, but my favorite is *The Ed Sullivan Show*. He's the king. I'll never forget when he had Elvis Presley on. Man, he was amazing! Can you believe he got drafted into the army?"

"What a loss...at least we can look forward to his comeback, right?" Charles said.

"Remember when those stupid teachers at school told us not to watch the Elvis show because he was so vulgar?" Elizabeth said.

"Yeah, they wouldn't even show his entire body. They filmed him from the waist up. What a joke!" Charles said.

"Of course, you realize the main reason most of the kids at school watched it was because they told us not to," Anna said. "My dad constantly watches *Gunsmoke*. I don't understand why guys love those shows about cowboys and gunfights. Mom and I used to watch *I Love Lucy* all the time, but then we got hooked on that quiz show, *Twenty-One*. Have any of you seen it?"

"I heard that was fixed," I said.

"No way! You mean they cheat?"

"Yeah, they cheat. Our dad is convinced that if the producers like a guy on the show, they'll give him the answers to help him win," Charles said.

"It must be fixed. I can't imagine anyone knowin' so much pointless stuff," Elizabeth said. I did not really hear what she said. I was too busy staring at her belly button, which she revealed by tying her T-shirt in a knot.

"Well, Mom and I like it. I hope it stays on." Suddenly, I saw two shadows standing in the doorway. It was Jack and Drew. They looked like two outlaws entering a saloon.

"Okay suckers, enough of the small talk. Ya ready to do this or what?" Jack asked.

"Ready whenever you are movie star," Charles replied.

"Why don't you boys take this outside before it gets ugly," Anna added.

"Hit a home run for me, Chris!" Elizabeth said.

"I'll hit two." My heart pounded against my chest. Was she toying with me or did I really have a glimmer of hope? She flirted with me all the time when we were younger, but this was different.

"Wow. You really do set your goals high, don't you?" she said, smiling.

"You'll see. I have a few surprises left in me," I said. I could not believe what I was saying. It was like a whole other person was doing the talking for me. I was flirting with one of the prettiest girls in school and getting away with it. Maybe she did see me as all grown-up. Charles grounded me with a quick glance. I grabbed my hat and glove and headed out into the backyard. It was time to do battle.

SIX

"The great man is he who does not lose his child's heart."

MENCIUS

Every Funball game starts out the same. Jack stands in the batter's box. That's right, he painted an area on the lawn where the batter on deck stands. He takes off his hat and cues Drew. You have to see this to truly believe it. Drew bucks up and sings, with his shaky voice, every word of the National Anthem. Charles and I crack up when he tries to hit the high note, "...the land and of the freeeee!" Then he yells out, "Play ball!" Jack puts his hat back on and takes the field.

We were all pretty good baseball players. We played on the school team in Junior High. Charles and I set a school record for turning the most double plays in a season. Jack's speed earned him a position in centerfield and Drew put his stocky frame behind home plate as catcher. We finished second in our league. So you see, Funball was just a way of fooling around.

What is Funball? Perhaps the most important part of the game is the ball itself. It's a red, hard plastic ball that soars through the air when you hit it just right. If we used a baseball, too many windows would get broken so we used the funball instead. When you get a hold of one with a swing of the bat you feel like Superman.

Because we only play with two people on each team, we do not have to run when we hit the ball. There are landmarks all over the field, telling us how to give credit for each hit. Any ball hit on the ground past the pitcher is a single. The lilac bushes down the right-field line mark a double. A ball hit to the shed out in deep right earns you a triple and any ball hit past it is a home run. Each team gets two outs an inning. Every game is six innings. Much of the excitement comes from home runs or great defensive plays.

Then there are the monuments. Yankee Stadium has monuments of players like Babe Ruth and Lou Gehrig that are actually on the field. Jack's yard also had its own little monument section. The first one worth mentioning is Humphrey's house out in left field. Humphrey is a basset hound pooch my uncle bought for Jack's tenth birthday. Not far from the doghouse, closer to center, is the birdbath my aunt and uncle love to stare at. Next to the shed in right, there is a small rock with a white "B" painted on it. This is where Jack buried his Brooklyn Dodgers hat when they moved to Los Angeles. Last, but not least, was the weeping willow in dead center we affectionately called "Big Babe."

The orange, yellow, and red leaves let us know it was World Series time again. The smell of a fire warming a nearby chimney filled the air. We were surrounded by the ingredients of a perfect fall day.

Charles and I batted first and started the ribbing right away as part of our strategy to get under Jack's skin.

"It's a good thing we don't have to run in this game, Jack, 'cause you'd never be able to throw us out with that little rag arm you got."

"Never mind my weak, little arm, Charles. Concentrate on gettin' some fly balls out here, big shot! I'm gonna catch everything in a ten mile radius of where I'm standin'."

"Did I hear you say ten mile radius? When did we start talkin' about the size of Drew's ass?" I said.

"Hey, just remember this. There are winners in this world and losers and Mr. Chris 'I'll never get a date with Elizabeth Allen no matter how hard I try' Thomas just so happens to be on the loser side." That one hurt.

"All right, fatboy. Let's get this game started. The barbecue's callin' and I wanna play before you run off to stuff your face," I said. Drew was not really fat, but when he stood next to scrawny Jack he looked a little portly. He was easy to tease.

We played for quite a while without too much ribbing. Charles and I were able to get some good hits early on. I usually get a lot of the singles and doubles and then Charles hits the long ball and scores all the ghost runners.

Jack tried to catch up with one of Charles's screamers early on, but he ran into the birdbath. We knew it would not be long before he would unleash a fury of anger on it. The ball dropped in for a grand slam. Charles celebrated by taking a victory lap. This infuriated Jack, especially since there were no bases. He vented his anger by pulling twigs off of "Big Babe." He usually had quite a pile by the end of the game.

We finished the top of the first inning after scoring eight runs. Then it was Jack and Drew's turn. Jack caught fire early and hit two home runs off of me with ghost runners on base. The most exciting part of the inning came with two ghost runners on and Drew up at the plate with one out. The score was tied and they wanted to get the lead. He fouled off a few pitches and then I made a mistake. I put one right over the plate. Drew hit it a mile.

"You'll never catch it! That's way outta here! You got no chance!" Jack shouted.

Just as Charles made it to the tree, the funball hit the top branch of "Big Babe." With all its energy sapped, it began to fall.

I shouted orders at Charles, "It's comin' down, get under it, it's comin' right at you!" The ball bounced around the branches like it was in a pinball machine. Charles turned left, then right, then left again. As he went to turn one last time, he fell to the ground.

"It's gonna drop in!" Drew shouted.

While Charles lay flat on his back, he made a last-second attempt, stretching as far as he could. Wouldn't you know, that beautiful, little red gumdrop fell right into his glove.

"I don't believe it!" Drew said as he fell to the ground. I don't remember hearing Jack yell. I think he was over in the corner of the yard, kicking up all his mother's flowers in her garden. He would pay for it later when his father came home.

"That was the greatest catch ever! That's my big brother!" I shouted. I ran out to help him up. We laughed at the drama and luck of the play. When we had Jack's attention, I knelt down next to Charles and we both made the sign of the cross like we were saying a prayer, thanking God. Jack was so steamed he went back to the garden for round two. We waited a few minutes for him to stop swearing at the flowers and then the game continued.

The exciting plays went back and forth for the next few innings. The next memorable play came when I hit a weak pop-up Drew ran after.

"No way! You'll never get it! No chance," I said. Jack could not control his excitement.

"Dive for it, fat ass!"

Drew stretched out his glove and pulled the ball in. What a catch! Of course, then he stumbled and fell, wiping out the family grill. He made Jack apologize for the "fat ass" remark before we resumed play. Later on in the game, I played the outfield and Charles pitched. I wanted to get revenge against Drew for making that catch.

"Hey, Charles, did you see Kathy in the cafeteria at school yesterday?" I said. Drew had a crush on this girl since second grade. She loved to lead him on. It sort of drove us all nuts, but I had to use it during Funball.

"Yeah, I saw her. She looked real nice, didn't she?"

"Oh, yeah. Ya know, I hear she's thinkin' about askin' you to the sock hop comin' up next week," I said.

"Cool. I don't really like her that much, but I hear she's real friendly, if ya know what I mean."

"Shut up and pitch!" Drew shouted.

"Drew could never go out with her. She'd never date a guy with a girl's name. Hey, Andrea, why don't you just give it up and start buyin' women's clothes like dresses and bras. In fact, you look like you could use a bra right now," I said.

"After this home run I'll show you who needs a bra." Charles threw it and Drew hit it. I watched from centerfield as this thing went off his bat. It went higher and higher.

"That's gonna clear 'Big Babe!' It's got a chance," Jack shouted.

Charles and I did not even move. We looked up and watched it carry right over "Big Babe." Even though the home run killed us, we could not help but marvel at the spectacle. I walked in to the mound to talk to Charles.

"Maybe we oughta lay off Kathy, huh?"

"Good idea."

We got back at them in our own way. After Drew's home run, Jack came up to bat and Charles hit him square in the back with the ball. It did not hurt him, but it was our way of saying we were not going down easy. Of course, to truly make the game authentic like the major leagues, Jack had to charge the mound. He ran out and flipped Charles onto his back and then I ran in and slapped him around until Drew knocked me over. We wrestled around for a bit.

We knew we needed to start playing harder or we would lose the game for sure. On the next pitch, Drew hit a blazing line-drive out into right field. I got a good jump on it. Charles shouted to let me know I was running out of room. There was a line of bushes all along the right-field wall. Without thinking, I jumped up in the air, caught the ball, and went right over the bushes and out of sight by the road.

"It's about time you losers got two outs," Jack said. Charles ran over to help me up.

"That was for you, big brother. I could tell you were gettin' a little edgy. Now let's go score some runs." A black '58 Dodge Royal was parked at the end of the street. We did not notice it at the time because we were too focused on winning the game. Charles's bat and my mouth went to work; we put on quite a show in the last inning.

Charles's home run pulled us within three. Jack's temper was up again. That poor tree lost a few more branches. He looked like a tornado, spinning all around, destroying everything in his path. Then, with the tying run at the plate, Charles hit a ball harder than any before. We thought for sure it was a home run. To our amazement, Jack gave chase and caught it in full stride, robbing him of a homer.

"Are you kiddin' me?" Charles dropped the bat in defeat.

"What d'ya think of that, boys? We got some defense too, huh?" Drew said. Jack collapsed and lay there, savoring the moment. He killed our momentum, but we were not through yet. We had one out left. We waited while Drew carried Jack around the field on his shoulders.

"Autographs? Anyone want an autograph of the greatest Funball player ever?"

"Not now, Drew, my fans ask too much of me. I'm only one man even though I play like two."

Just as I walked up to bat I noticed some commotion on the back porch. It was Elizabeth and Anna.

"Hey, Chris, ya gonna hit a home run for me?" Elizabeth asked.

"I'll do my best," I said. Talk about pressure, then I had to hit one. She was watching. If I got out, the game was over and Charles and I would be big losers. I flexed my muscles to get the blood flowing. My hands felt numb. It was my big moment to shine.

"Hey, Chris, ya gonna hit a home run for me?" Drew said in a mock-female voice.

"You do that well, Andrea. Now you have a voice to go with your name," I said.

Drew pitched one low and outside just how I like it and I connected. It soared way out past the monuments in right field. Jack could not even try to catch up with it. The score was all tied up. The girls gave me a cheer, "Chris, Chris, he's our man. If he can't do it, no one can!"

Elizabeth and Anna were whispering and smiling at me. Maybe she did look at me differently since I became a big freshman with serious muscles, well—muscles. I tried not to look over at the girls, but I made every move with Elizabeth in mind. I threw in all kinds of extra stretching and flexing and I even spit a few times just to look extra tough. She could not take her eyes off of me. My confidence soared.

After a couple of hits, we had two ghost runners on with one out left in the top of the last inning of the game. A base hit would put us in the lead.

"All right, Drew...enough kiddin' around. Let's end this game. Get him out!" Jack said.

"This is it, Charles. Remember that if you get out, you and your brother are chumps and we win," Drew said.

"You boys sound like you're gettin' nervous," I said.

"You kiddin'? We have the greatest defense in the world. In fact, I'm so confident Drew is gonna get Charles out here, I'll declare that we don't even need our last ups."

"What? No last ups? You wanna make that official?" Charles jumped at the opportunity, knowing Jack's mouth continuously got him into trouble. Drew started sweating.

"You got it! It's official. We forfeit our last ups! Drew and I don't need to swing a bat at one more pitch. If you guys score here, we lose." I turned to Charles.

"Well, 'Carpe Diem' my friend...'Seize the Day,'" I said.

The girls ran down onto the sidelines for a closer look. Charles stared down Drew as he approached the plate. Drew wound up and delivered the pitch. Charles hit it high and deep to left. Jack dodged the birdbath, running as fast as he could. He closed in on the ball as it dropped. A tiny smile came to his face as it came closer and closer to his glove.

"You got it, Jack! Catch it!" Drew shouted, but in a split second his hopes were dashed. "Wait! Look out for the..." Before Drew could finish his sentence, Jack ran right into the doghouse, waking up poor Humphrey. He fell flat on his back. The ball landed safely for a home run. We were champions.

We went to see if Jack was okay and then we celebrated with the girls. Drew leaned over and delicately said, "Jack...you okay? You gave it everything you had." Jack jumped up and pushed Drew back. Then he grabbed the doghouse, which was almost as tall as he was, and tipped it over. We fell on the ground laughing as Jack proceeded to flip the doghouse over and over again with poor Humphrey in it. We knew the pooch would not get hurt, but he sure looked confused when he started rolling around the yard like he was in a clothes drier.

While everyone was focused on Jack, Elizabeth walked over to me. She took advantage of the distraction, grabbed my hand, and dragged me up to the house. I did not know what she was up to.

"What are you doin', Elizabeth? Why'd you want me to come up here?"

"Don't say a word, just trust me." We ran into the garage where my uncle's car rested. He had the coolest '57 Chevy Corvette around. It had a red leather interior, shiny chrome fenders, fresh red paint on the exterior, and a white streak down the side. I can still see the New York State license plate, VFC-719. She grabbed the keys and opened the passenger door.

"What are you doin'? Are you crazy? My uncle loves this car. He'll kill us if he finds out." I began to panic.

"The only thing I know is that I'm crazy about you," she said. Corny lines like that actually work when uttered by a beauty like Elizabeth Allen. We both jumped in. "C'mon, let's take her for a ride. What d'ya say?" She held out the keys. My heart nearly jumped out of my chest. I did not have my license, but I moved my dad's car in and out of the driveway all the time. I thought I could probably handle my uncle's car, if I was insane enough to try.

"Let's go!" I said as I grabbed the keys, started her up, and crept out of the driveway without anyone knowing. Then I let it rip. We opened all the windows and flew down the road. Elizabeth looked incredible with the breeze blowing through her hair.

"This is the coolest car I've ever been in," she said.

"Yeah, my uncle's got good taste. I'm gonna own a car like this someday."

"Wow, first a home run and then a ride in this cool machine...you're full of all kinds of surprises, aren't you? I can't wait to see what's next." She ran her fingers through my hair. I pulled into this little parking lot behind an old, abandoned movie house. I cut off the engine and turned toward her. Our eyes met. This was my chance. I needed to move and move quickly. I pushed her hair over her shoulder to clear a path to her face. My hand gently brushed against her cheek. This was the moment I had dreamed of.

"What are we doin' here?" she said with a wicked smile.

"I don't know...I just thought that...maybe we could..." Before I finished my sentence, she grabbed my face and kissed me. I melted like an ice cube on a radiator. As my nerves settled down, I slipped my right arm around her back and pulled her toward me. I never felt lips so soft. In fact, I had never felt lips—period. She was my first kiss—on the lips, that is. Unless of course, you count my neighbor when I was three, but I don't remember liking it very much.

I savored every moment. Sliding my hand up the back of her neck, I pulled her closer to me. She reached over and put her right arm around my body and touched my back. Her moves were gentle and deliberate. She threw her head back for a moment and I kissed her neck.

We were movie stars sharing a romantic scene. I could not believe I was getting away with this—a home run, a cool car, and a beautiful girl. That little, pudgy kid was history. I had finally arrived.

Her hair smelled like heaven. I thought about all the times in school I had longed to touch it. I used to lay in bed at night and fantasize about pressing my lips against hers. I could not believe it was happening for real. My left hand landed on her right knee. She let out a few subtle noises as I moved it slowly up the outside of her warm, left thigh. I was pretty sure that was the way the movie stars did it.

Her pulse raced when my hand squeezed her leg—what an amazing piece of God's work. She was like a Michelangelo statue. Her mouth tasted fresh and fruity. She never opened her eyes. I know because I kept opening mine to see if she was opening hers. I continued to move my hand up her thigh. She stopped me at her hip.

"No, Chris. That's enough. We'd better stop now." She took a deep breath and pushed me away. My entire body was glowing. I did not want to stop. I could have sat there in that car and kissed her for hours. It was kind of scary because I did not really know what to do after my hand moved up to her hip. To be honest, I was just trying to imitate the guys I saw in the movies. I had some idea what came next, but I definitely was not ready for that...at least not in my uncle's car. I was so lost in this world I did not even notice that the black '58 Dodge Royal slowly passed by us, stopped for a moment, and then drove away.

I was able to get a few more kisses before she put a stop to all of our role-playing and said we should head back before anyone noticed we were gone. For a moment I did not think I could drive. I felt too lightheaded. I was floating. Somehow, I managed to steer the Corvette back into the garage. As we jumped out of the car, I put my fingers under her chin, drew her to me, and gave her one last kiss.

"You're amazing. You know that? I've had a crush on you for years, but I never thought I had a chance with you," I said.

"You've grown up a lot in the past few years, Christopher Thomas. I remember when you couldn't even ride a bike." She laughed.

"Yeah, like that was yesterday. I'm almost fifteen, Elizabeth. It's time you start taking me seriously." Just then Drew walked in with Anna and Charles.

"What's goin' on, guys? Is it safe to come in?" he said.

"Of course, stupid," Elizabeth said. She was blushing. I made Elizabeth Allen blush! I beamed with pride. I felt cooler than the King of Rock 'N' Roll himself.

Charles walked over and whispered in my ear, "You took the car, didn't ya?" I nodded. "I wanna hear all about it later."

"Hey, Drew, can you go see if that foolish brother of mine is done torturing that poor dog."

"Sure," he said, heading for the backyard.

The paperboy walked up the driveway. I recognized him immediately. His name was Benjamin. He came from a good family so I always joked around with him when we ran into each other in the neighborhood.

"Hey, Benjamin, what's the word on the street?" I asked.

"Your uncle has a really cool '57 Chevy Corvette." He stared wide-eyed at the machine.

"Is that right? Well, maybe someday I'll get him to take you and your brother, out for a spin."

"That'd be great! Take it easy," he said as he handed me a rolled-up newspaper and walked away.

"Say hello to your parents for me." I opened the paper and read the headlines. I froze as I saw that face that was all too familiar. The headline read "Crazy Man Escapes from Mental Institution!"

SEVEN

"Nothing great was ever achieved without enthusiasm."
                                            RALPH WALDO EMERSON

After a half hour of throwing the doghouse around, Jack could no longer lift his arms. As soon as poor Humphrey was able to stand, he took two steps and barfed all over the place. He looked like he just got off of a roller coaster at Coney Island. When Jack was completely cooled off, we played Ping-Pong and Billiards down in his game room. My aunt made pizza. While we were eating, the issue of the newspaper headlines popped up again.

"So, Chris, what's the story behind this guy in the newspaper?" Elizabeth asked.

"Believe me, you don't wanna know," Charles said.

"C'mon guys, what's the big deal? Tell us the story," Drew said.

"Okay, but if I tell you the story it's not my fault if you're too scared to go to sleep tonight," I said, waiting to see if Charles wanted me to tell it. I knew I could do a great job. It was just what I needed to seal the deal with Elizabeth. I proved I was athletic and romantic. It was time to show her my entertaining and funny side.

"Oh, this'll be fun. Halloween is right around the corner. It's a perfect time for scary stories. Wait! Let me turn the lights out," Anna said.

"How're we gonna eat the pizza if we can't see it, you twit?" Jack said.

"Don't yell at me, 'Mr. Grumpy.' I'll light a candle."

"Oh, perfect. This'll be really scary. Chris, do you mind if I sit next to you? I get awfully frightened by spooky stories," Elizabeth said.

"Of course, I don't mind. Slide over here." She locked her arm around mine, and moved in close. I wished we were alone again. Anna joined us on the couch while the boys lounged in the chairs. The room was almost completely black. Scattered pieces of pizza surrounded a red candle lit in the center of the coffee table. It flickered underneath my face, giving me a ghostlike presence.

I love telling stories even more than doing impressions, especially when trying to impress a beautiful girl like Elizabeth. I began in a low, quiet voice to enhance the ghoulish atmosphere. "About three years ago...something happened...that changed us forever. It was a cold, dark night a week before Christmas. Charles and I were playin' in the snow with our friends: Nick, Porter, and Goodie. A blizzard hit the night before and dropped a couple feet of snow on us. We were outside, clownin' around and pushin' each other into the huge snow banks. All of us teamed up against Porter 'cause he kept puttin' snow down our pants." Everyone laughed. I felt Elizabeth's breath on my right cheek.

"Just as we were pilin' on top of him, we heard this commotion down the street. About a hundred yards away, this man was jumpin' up and down and actin' all crazy. He was walkin' back and forth in the middle of the road and shoutin' out obscenities which, at that age, I had only heard spoken by my cousin, Jack, here." Jack sat in the corner, looking sheepish.

"We noticed some people on the porch of the house right in front of him. They yelled a few things back at him and then went inside. Goodie looked at me, paused and said, 'I'm outta here,' and he ran into our house. We called him a chicken, but then we all followed him inside." I jiggled the ice in my glass to make the soda pop nice and cold.

"What happened to him? Was he really crazy?" Drew asked.

"Relax 'Shirley,' let him continue with the story," Jack scolded.

"So, like I was sayin', we all went inside. Now, you have to remember this was a while ago. We were all little kids and we loved playin' this game with my dad called 'The Monster.'" Charles smiled in remembrance.

"This was our favorite game of all time. The way it worked was we turned all the lights out in the house and hid upstairs. We hid in closets, under beds, behind dressers, you name it. My dad used tape to make his face look all distorted. He taped his nose straight up, one eye down, one eye over, and his lower lip all crooked." I modeled these terrible faces for Elizabeth. She cringed and squeezed my arm.

"When we were all set, he'd slowly walk up the stairs. The suspense alone chilled our blood. Just as he got to the top, he'd turn on a flashlight under his chin. We'd all scream in terror at the

45

grotesque 'Monster.' Then he'd turn off the light and sneak quietly around the rooms. It was really scary."

"We all loved that game. Dad made it a lot of fun," Charles said. "The best part was when he grabbed someone in the dark. Whoever he got, screamed insanely while everyone else ran. Sometimes he'd take the kid downstairs and pretend to put him in a dungeon."

"One time he tricked us all real bad. He put his shoes around the corner of the door. We all were convinced that he was standin' there until he came up behind us and grabbed Mary and me. I loved it, but she kicked and screamed like you couldn't believe," I said.

"What about the guy outside?"

"Drew, would you cool your jets? He's gettin' to it, be patient," Jack said.

"So, this night we were playin' the game, my mom kept sayin' we should stop before somebody got hurt. She always had a sixth sense about things. Of course, we ignored her. Then Dad grabbed Goodie and the little guy completely lost it."

"Yeah, Goodie almost lost it all right...in his pants," Charles said. They loved that one.

"Seriously though, Goodie couldn't stop screamin'. Dad kept sayin', 'Goodie it's okay, it's just me, it's only a game,' but Goodie couldn't pull out of it and Dad's grotesque face didn't help. We had to turn all the lights on and take the tape off of Dad's face. Goodie eventually calmed down. Everything was very peaceful and then suddenly, a bright light flashed in our bedroom window."

"What was it? Some kind of spaceship?" Anna asked.

"Charles ran over, opened the window, and stuck his head out into the crisp, December air. We all ran to the window to see what was goin' on. As I approached him, this huge beam of light shone on his face. He jumped back from the window."

"What was it? What happened?" Elizabeth said, grabbing me tighter.

"My father ran over to the window and slammed it shut. Mom yelled out, 'Jerry, get down here. There's somethin' goin' on out there.' We all ran downstairs. My father pulled his shotgun out of the hall closet for extra effect. He said, 'Nobody is gonna mess with my family, I'll tell you that right now!' This, of course, scared the livin' daylights out of all of us," I said. I paused and took a sip of my drink.

"Tell 'em 'bout all the lights," Charles said.

"When we got downstairs there were more lights. The light that frightened Charles was a spotlight from a helicopter. It was flyin' up and down our street, searchin' for somethin'. We all ran over to the window to see what was goin' on. Five police cars drove down our street, chased by an ambulance. My mother kept tryin' to calm everybody down, but 'The Monster' game had us all wound up and then every little thing frightened us."

"I know how that is. That's like when you watch a scary movie and then you suddenly notice all the little, creepy noises in the house," Anna said.

"Tell us what was really goin' on," Drew said.

"Okay. While we were playin' in the street earlier, this 'crazy' guy went into his parents' home for a Christmas party. We learned from some neighbors that his father tormented him a lot when he was little. Anyway, at the party, everyone was opening gifts and enjoyin' the holiday spirit until this guy offered a gift to his father. Everyone gathered around as the father carefully took the bow, ribbon, and paper off of his present. Instead of findin' a nice tie or a set of screwdrivers he found, wrapped neatly in the box...a human heart!"

"No way! That's gross!" Drew shouted.

"He calmly told his father he had given him a heart 'cause he never had one of his own. While everyone stood there in shock, the son went into the garage and reappeared, carrying the family axe. He held it high and lunged toward his father."

"Get outta town! That's scary as hell!" Jack said. He and Drew pulled their chairs closer to the couch. We were all sitting very close together except for Charles who kept his distance. The candle illuminated the room and made everyone's face glow.

"Some of the guests wrestled him to the ground and threw him out of the house. Now picture this. This 'madman' was outside screamin' nasty things and holdin' an axe. While only about a hundred yards away, five little kids were playin' in the snow...us, right? We got scared and ran into the house. Unfortunately, there were three young teenage girls who were out walkin' off a big holiday dinner. As they approached him, he

47

pulled out the axe and started chasin' 'em." I demonstrated on Elizabeth. She screamed and buried her head in my chest.

"He started chasin' 'em. Remember there was about three feet of snow from the big storm. The three young girls split up. The tallest one went left, the middle one went right, but the shortest one ran straight. She was the one he pursued. They ran to the end of the street and into the snow. The young girl ran as fast as her little legs would move. The guy gained on her. Just after they turned the corner of the big, white house at the end of the street, she fell."

"Damn it! Don't they always fall?" Jack said.

"The man lunged at her and buried the axe in the back of her leg."

"No way! Oh, my God!" Anna said.

"Then this guy sorta got confused. He grabbed the axe, jumped up, and started runnin' through the backyards of our neighborhood. He didn't know where he was or where he was goin'. He just lost it. He ran wildly all over the place. He decided to hide the axe and then try to run away before the police showed up. Where would he hide? He was probably looking for a house where no one was home...in other words...a house that was...pitch-black."

"Who had the only dark house on the block? Remember that the whole time this was goin' on, our entire house was pitch-black because we were playin 'The Monster,'" Charles said.

"Oh my God, what if 'The Madman' snuck into your house and you guys thought he was 'The Monster?'" Anna said. That spooked everyone in the room.

"That's a good point. I'll tell you somethin' that's even scarier. My mom and Goodie's mom put on their coats and boots and walked to the end of the street to ask the police officers what was happenin'. What if they were taken as hostages? In fact, the next day we saw the guy's footprints in our own backyard...they went right up to our back door. The cops caught him just two doors down from our house," I said.

"The worst part was that Chris and I delivered newspapers to all the people on the block. Believe me—that was one route no paperboy in town wanted. I'm gonna get another soda pop. Does anybody want one?" Charles asked on his way out of the room. Everyone was too engrossed in the story to respond.

"I was terrified every day we had to deliver papers after that happened. I kept thinkin' that it could've been us. I can still see the footprints, the bloody snow, and the police tape that marked off the crime scene. Our neighbor got quite the shock when she saw her dog sniffing around the backyard the next day. There was a disturbance in the snow by her flower bed. She nearly fainted when her pooch dug up the bloody axe."

"What happened to the girl? Did she die?" Elizabeth asked.

"Oh, I almost forgot. She pulled herself together with all her strength and crawled to a home nearby where her friend was babysitting. By then, her other two friends had already called the cops and they were on their way. Believe it or not, she did survive, but she'll never walk normal again. Charles and I saw her at a football game not too long ago."

"Well, all I know is you better not come ringin' the doorbell and collapsin' on me when I'm babysittin', oh, darling brother of mine," Anna said, throwing a pillow at Jack.

"Yeah, I could just see you. What did you do now, you fool? Mom and Dad are gonna kill you!" We all laughed.

"That's why I froze when I saw the newspaper today. It says that this guy escaped from the mental institution. If you read on a little further, it also says he swore if he ever broke free he'd go back and kill his father. Remember, that's how the whole thing started," I said.

"Did the parents move off of your street?" Drew asked.

"No. They're still just a hundred yards away."

"I'd move. That's it, move. No way in hell would I still be livin' on that street," Jack said. Everyone sat in silence for a moment.

"It's gettin' dark outside. It looks kinda creepy out there, huh? Well, Charles and I should be headin' out. Elizabeth, have fun walkin' home," I said.

"Wait one minute, Christopher Thomas! If you think I'm gonna walk home alone you're as crazy as that guy in the story!" Suddenly, she pulled me down onto the couch again, "Oh my God! Everybody get down. Look!" She pointed to the window at the back door. We all hit the floor. We saw the shadow of a man outside the window.

"Aw God! It's the guy. Knowin' my luck, it's gotta be that crazy bastard. He heard us talkin' about him and he's gonna kill us," Jack said. He crouched down behind his chair.

"I'm gonna go take a look," I said as I got up.

"Are you nuts? Don't go over there. I'm scared," Elizabeth whimpered.

"Don't worry. What could happen? I'm just gonna take a look." I crept over and peeked through the window. I did not see anything so I slowly opened the door.

"Chris, what are you doin'?" Anna whispered.

I took one step outside the door and looked all around. Then I tried to calm the others.

"See, there's nobody out here." Just as Elizabeth came over toward me, an arm reached out and grabbed me around the neck. I shrieked in terror as I got pulled off to the side and out of their view.

"Chris!" Drew jumped to his feet and came after me. They all ran to the doorway to see what had happened. Charles and I stood there with our arms around each other's shoulder. We pointed at them and said, "Gotcha!"

~ EIGHT ~

"The life which is unexamined is not worth living."

PLATO

After Charles and I walked Elizabeth home, she and I stood at her front door for a few moments and then I gave her a kiss good night. She had every opportunity to ask me to the big dance, but she never did. I was satisfied with all I got anyway. My stock at school was sure to rise when everybody heard about us. Maybe she was going to ask me Monday at school. My fingers were crossed.

Charles laughed at me as I did my usual "wrap up" of the day's events. This is a habit I got from my mother. In an attempt to make the fun events of the day last longer, I usually do a summary of all the highlights. Charles always stops me and says, "Okay, here comes the wrap up, right?" While Charles was brushing his teeth, I reflected on the game, the story, and the prank we pulled on everybody.

After we finished our evening rituals of getting ready for bed, Charles hit the lights. We spent hours, over the years, talking in our little room. We talked about our ups and downs and worked out many of life's mysteries in that private confessional.

There is something enchanting about staring at the ceiling in a dark room when all you have to focus on is someone else's voice and the electrical impulses flashing in your brain. It is amazing how our thoughts could lead us in a million different directions. We never knew how these deep exchanges got started and we certainly never remembered how they ended. Somehow the two of us were able to talk about dozens of issues and people and still come back full circle to the topic where we began.

"I just can't seem to like that Elizabeth Allen very much," Charles said.

"I can't understand why. Ya think she's pretty, don't ya?"

"Sure, she's a knockout, but she has a history, Chris. She doesn't have the best reputation in town. Are you forgettin' she just dated Deke Marshall not long ago? Don't ya think that says somethin' about her? I just don't trust her."

51

"Yeah, but I don't care about all that stuff with Marshall. I think she's beautiful, exciting, and everything I want in a girl. Everyone around is dying to date her. Can you imagine what the guys will say when they find out I parked with her tonight? They'll flip!"

"Since when do you care what the guys think?"

"What d'ya mean?"

"You've been sayin' stuff like that a lot lately...about what the other guys think. Why do you care so much about what they think?"

"It's not that I care, but they'll be jealous when they find out I kissed the prettiest girl in school. Besides, it never hurts to make yourself a little bit more popular."

"What's that supposed to mean?"

"You know what I'm gettin' at."

"No, I don't. What d'ya mean?"

"It's just that sometimes I feel like no girl is ever gonna ask me to the Homecoming Dance and the guys will never let me live it down."

"Oh, come off it, Chris! You're crazy if you think you're the only kid in school who's worried about that. You need to remember that ten, even twenty or thirty years down the road, most of those people aren't even gonna be in your life. Remember to keep things in perspective."

"I know what you're sayin', but I just wish I was a little more popular, that's all. I wanna be the guy that all the girls wanna date and the guys wanna play ball with."

"Instead of focusing on what you think you don't have, concentrate on what you do. Think about it. When I threw that basketball tournament together at the park last summer, who got everyone cheerin' from the sidelines? Remember when you were chosen to represent the youth council at church and Father Kennedy had you read that speech at Mass? Who were all the parents talkin' about afterwards? And don't forget about all the times you get the guys laughin' over at Yorkie's Place. I bet if you asked anybody around the neighborhood what they thought of you, they'd only have good things to say."

"I appreciate what you're tryin' to do, but I just don't think people around here give me all that much credit. I'm not that important to them. If I were, I'd have a date to that stupid Homecoming Dance by now."

"So that's really botherin' you, huh? The Homecoming Dance? Well, I didn't wanna say anything, but I know for a fact that there are a couple of girls who are plannin' on askin' you to go with 'em," he said.

"Really? Where'd ya hear that?"

"Anna was tellin' me. By the way, she asked me to go with her."

"That's cool," I said. "Now you don't have to worry about gettin' a date."

"Yeah. I didn't feel like makin' it into a big deal anyway. Going with family alleviates the pressure."

"In all honesty though, I know you wanted to go with Carolyn Thomson. Why don't you ask her out some time? Everybody knows you're crazy about her," I said.

"Get outta here. Nobody thinks that. Besides, I'm not crazy about her."

"Charles, c'mon, who're you kiddin'? I'm your brother. You and I both know that every time we see her at church, you can't take your eyes off of her."

"Well, I think she's cute, but I just don't...I don't know."

"All I'm sayin' is you oughta ask her out. She comes from a good family. She's obviously pretty and talented. She must be smart because she's always on the Honor Roll they post in the church lobby. I don't know...she sounds pretty good to me."

There was a moment or two of a pause and then Charles asked, "Ya really think she's pretty?"

"Seriously, I do. You two would definitely look good together."

"I don't know, we'll see."

At that point we heard our dad coming down the hall. He used to check in on us, periodically, to see if we were really asleep in bed or just staying up late talking. As we heard his footsteps approaching, we immediately became silent and buried our heads under our pillows.

The door opened. The hall light lit up a small area of the room. Dad stood there and observed for a few seconds. If we were silent and motionless long enough, he would close the door and leave. If we were not able to feign sleep, he would yell at us for staying up so late. We pulled it off nicely that night. We waited for about ten seconds after he shut the door to make sure he was gone and then we resumed our conversation.

"So are ya gonna tell me what happened with Elizabeth or not?" Charles asked.

"Yeah, she talked me into takin' Uncle Bobby's car out for a spin."

"I knew it! You're nuts! You barely even know how to drive!"

"I know. You woulda been proud of me. I drove it all the way down to the old movie house on Main Street and parked it in the back. We sat there and made out for a while." Even in the dark, Charles could tell I was grinning from ear to ear.

"I can't believe it. What got into you? I know she used to flirt with you when you were little, but I thought that was all just for fun. You took Uncle Bobby's car without permission and drove to Main Street and back? So, how far did ya get with her?"

"We kissed for a while and I put my hand on her thigh. You can't believe how incredible her body is. She is in perfect shape...not an ounce of fat on her, but she's not skinny or anything. She's shapely and soft. You can't even imagine."

"I can imagine," Charles said. "How 'bout the kiss?"

"Soft...warm...passionate..."

"Okay, okay, I get it. You enjoyed the kiss. D'ya think she's gonna ask you to the dance or what?"

"It would be a dream come true. The whole thing seems like a dream; it's completely surreal. Kissin' in a parked car is one thing, but d'ya really think she'd risk her reputation by goin' with me? What would people say? I mean, am I really cool enough to be Elizabeth Allen's date to the dance?"

"Did you not hear me say she dated Deke Marshall? Chris, she's not royalty for cryin' out loud. You're ten times the guy Marshall is. I still say any girl that'd go out with him isn't worth it, but you don't wanna listen to me so I guess you'll have to find out for yourself."

"We'll see. I don't even know why we're talkin' about it. She probably won't ask me anyway. Besides, everybody who's anybody goes to Murphy's big bash after the Homecoming Dance, right? I wouldn't know what to do with that crowd. I'd be so nervous."

"There's nothin' to be nervous about. Remember I went to one last year? It's not that big of a deal. Everyone makes it out to be the greatest event in world history. It's just another stupid party."

"What was it like?"

"It was okay. Murphy holds it down in this musty, old basement he thinks is cool because his parents added some rugs and furniture. The problem is that nobody acts like themselves. They're all so concerned with how they look in front of everyone else that they all act phony as hell. There'll be one group of kids makin' out in one corner of the room, a group sharin' smokes in another corner, and one group who aren't sure what they wanna do, standin' right in the middle. Oh, yeah, I almost forgot to mention, just about everyone gets completely smashed."

"What do they drink? Beer or harder stuff?"

"They drink beer mostly and whatever is left in Old Man Murphy's liquor cabinet. It's really stupid, Chris. I don't know why it's such a big deal."

"I know, I know. You and I have had this discussion many times. Don't worry about me. I'm not gonna get into all that stuff. I'm perfectly happy tellin' my stories and doin' my impressions. If people ask, I'll just say I'm not drinkin' and leave it at that," I said.

"I hope so, little brother. Believe me, it's not easy to stand out from the rest of the crowd. I've done it for a while and you certainly won't be able to do it if you don't get rid of that 'I want everybody to like me' attitude. If we do end up goin' there, just stay close to me. If I'm not drinkin' either, it'll be easier for you to dodge everybody."

"I just hope it's not an issue."

"Look, don't get all stressed out. Remember Dad always taught you to be your own man. Don't let anyone bully you into doin' somethin' you don't wanna do," he said.

"Hey, if Porter goes he won't be drinkin', right? I can hang out with him too. I don't think we can count on Nick. He'll get carried away by his football buddies, especially after a tough Homecoming game. Let's see, who else is there? Goodie probably won't go at all and I think Jack and Drew said they need to get up early on Sunday so they're gonna skip it. Well, the numbers aren't in our favor, but at least we'll have each other to fall back on. Hey, why doesn't Porter drink?"

"I think it has somethin' to do with his old man, but I don't know the whole story and I don't know if I ever wanna," he said. We lay there in silence for a few moments, reflecting on all of those monumental issues. Charles used to say he could never fully grasp why so many kids felt the pressure to drink and smoke just because everyone else was doing it. He was definitely ahead of his years. He always called alcohol the "Golden Crutch." He said people drank because they simply did not feel confident enough in themselves. They needed to feel a little buzz before they could talk to a girl they liked or act cool in front of their friends.

I could not admit it to my brother, but I was feeling a great deal of pressure. I did not really know what I would do if I was with Elizabeth and she wanted me to drink. How could I say no? I liked her too much. I could not offend her. Besides, everyone would think I was a wimp if I did not join in. I would never recover from that. My future at Wilson High would be over.

I tried to change the subject, "I can't wait for school on Monday. I'll probably see Elizabeth right after fourth period; we have lunch together. I really hope she asks me."

"Just remember you don't need to drink to feel confident, you don't need to smoke to be cool, and you don't need a date with Elizabeth Allen to belong. I'm sure once you get a date to the dance you'll loosen up. Who knows, you may share a dance with some beautiful girl who will end up changin' your life." Charles's voice faded as he began to doze off. My eyes had closed as well and my thoughts of being with Elizabeth in that car soothed my worries.

As Charles faded he uttered one last phrase, "I just can't seem to like that Elizabeth Allen very much." With romance on my mind, Saturday had come to a close.

Sundays were always relaxing. After finishing breakfast, we took turns reading the newspaper. My father had finished it from cover to cover by that time, but I had to find ways of sharing with my other siblings. Mary wanted to read about the polka dot fashion craze, I had to check the movie listings for Brando's latest work, while Charles finished the sports article about all of the high school football match-ups. Then I ran upstairs and jumped into the shower.

Our house on a Sunday morning before church was always quite a sight. It was like watching the Marx Brothers dressed as firemen, getting ready to answer an emergency call. Having an entire family share a bathroom is insane. Two of the shorter people shared the sink, brushing their teeth, while two of the taller people combed their hair in the mirror over them, and another person was in the shower. Of course, you were never safe in the shower because my dad always loved to fill up a cup of cold water and dump it on whoever was in there just to make them move a little faster. Then there would be a mad scramble to grab shoes and jackets and run out to the car before Dad pulled out of the driveway.

Believe it or not, I actually liked going to church on Sunday. Not really because of all the praying and singing and standing and kneeling, but because of all the people Charles and I used to make fun of. One time there was this guy sitting in front of us with a big gouge out of his ear. It looked like someone had actually taken a bite out of it. Of course, Charles could not let this go, so every time we sat down he would lean over and start chomping his teeth right next to the guy's ear. I know it sounds terrible, but we could not take everything seriously. My favorite routine was lip-synching when the cantor was singing the hymns. Charles thought this was hysterical because our church used to have this little old lady with a high, whiny voice.

One time I even remember my dad getting in on it. There was this little kid sitting in front of us who had this feathery blond hair that stuck straight up on the back of his head. Charles and I looked over and noticed Dad gently blowing on it and watching it sway in the wind like a weeping willow tree. My mother threw a fit that day.

Father Kennedy was the best priest of all time. He was always very friendly and approachable. He and my father talked sports after Mass while mom asked him about all the activities and events going on in the parish. His homilies were priceless. He would get up and tell a quick, little joke that had nothing to do with God or the Mass, but it always got everyone's attention before he began.

Charles and I served as altar boys. He would laugh at me before every Mass because I would always get nervous. I still don't know why. I guess I have always been something of a perfectionist, even at the age of ten.

I liked ringing the bell when the priest blessed the gifts. That was my role every week while Charles took care of lighting the candles. That always stressed me out because I was afraid I would make a mistake and burn the whole church down. We shared all the other duties.

We always did an excellent job. However, there was one time when Father Prior, the younger priest, turned to take the water and the wine from Charles and me and we were both bobbing up and down with laughter. He was good about it and said, "Tell me what's so funny after Mass."

What actually happened was this huge guy walked into the church and sat down right next to my mom. He had to be about six feet, eight inches tall. When they stood next to each other, Mom's head was right next to his waistline. A second before I had to ring the bell, Charles leaned over to me and said, "If that guy farts, he'll blow Mom's earrings right off her head." I tried to contain myself, but it was futile.

Everyone has been in the kind of situation when you cannot laugh because it is so quiet. Well, all that does is make you wanna laugh even more. I held it in as best as I could, but the more I held in the laughter, the more I bounced up and down in my seat. By the time I had to ring the bell I was squeaking and bouncing so much that the bell sounded like this pitiful, little jingle instead of a powerful ring. Although, it was a great time in my life, I was glad when Charles and I finally stopped being altar boys. It was a lot of work.

After Mass ended, our parents talked to their friends and Charles and I said hello to a few of our buddies. I tried to get Charles to go talk to Carolyn, but he was not up for it. Then it was back home for a big Italian dinner. As soon as we got home, Mom had the water boiling and the sauce bubbling. After sitting down to a wonderful meal, Charles and I spent the usual amount of time talking life over with our dad. Then it was on to our grandparents' house.

My grandmother had this beautiful, white, porcelain candy dish. Charles, Mary, and I would always look at each other until one of us had enough guts to lift the lid and take a peek. On a good day we would walk away with chocolate or peanuts. It's funny how little things like M&M's can make your day when you're a kid.

After spending time with family all day, it was back to our home where Dad made a fire and we sat around, listening to radio programs like *The Shadow* or *Lights Out*! Some nights we could hear the wind howling outside and see the snow blowing past the picture window like white powder. I remember feeling like that was the safest place in the world on those cold winter nights. I would get so excited about those wonderful stories while staring into the warm glow of the fire. I do not think it would have been nearly as special if I did not have my family with me to share it. As nine o'clock approached, the radio went off by Mom's orders and we all marched upstairs and got our clothes and work ready for Monday morning.

Charles and I went a couple more rounds of talking before we called it a night. He always teased me on Sunday night because I got tense about Mondays. One time he even got up and did a foolish dance to make me laugh before Christmas Break came to an end. That was rare for Charles. I guess I valued the holidays and weekends so much with my family and friends that I did not want them to end. Charles reminded me I should not be too down because the big Homecoming Dance was the following weekend and he was confident I would not be sitting home. It was amazing how "next weekend" sounded like such a far off place when uttered on a Sunday night.

NINE

"The ultimate measure of a man is not where he stands in moments of comfort, but where he stands at times of challenge & controversy."

MARTIN LUTHER KING, JR.

Monday morning rolled around soon enough and it was back to the rat race. Fortunately, I had something to look forward to. Thinking about seeing Elizabeth made it a little bit easier to get out of bed and face the dark, blue-black morning. I knew that day would go down as one of the most memorable in the history of Wilson High School—at least from my perspective.

I floated through my first few classes, carried by the delight of sharing my Elizabeth Allen story with just about anyone who would listen. When the fun was over I spent the rest of each class trying hard to keep my eyes open. I nodded off a few times during science. I never meant to fall asleep in class—it just happened. All I remembered afterward was staring at the teacher and then suddenly my eyes would feel really heavy. Suddenly, I was back in my warm, cozy bed at home. That is, until I heard my name called out by the teacher. I was not fully cognizant of the day's events until third period. That was when I had art with Ms. Matheson. I spent the majority of the class, like most boys, fantasizing about her.

This particular day we were all sitting around this huge table. There was a mannequin sitting in a beach chair that was wearing a Hawaiian shirt, a grass skirt, and a pair of sunglasses. A beach ball next to the chair capped off the "Tropical Theme" of the piece. I thought these were really corny, but I would never tell Ms. Matheson that. So with pad on desk and pencil in hand, I began to draw the image.

I do not remember at what point I began to make a total fool of myself, but I know this project did not keep me interested for very long. I focused on that ridiculous mannequin with the silly sunglasses. I stared deeper and deeper into that lifeless body and then unexpectedly my hormones kicked in. I cut all ties to this earth and I was soaring in my imagination again. Suddenly, those sunglasses slid down and a set of blue eyes stared back at me that could only be those of Ms. Matheson herself.

She looked great in that tacky Hawaiian shirt. She winked at me and said, "You're not paying attention are you, Chris? What's the matter, do I bore you? Am I not pretty enough for you?" She threw off her sunglasses and stood up. Her legs glistened in the hot sun as she began to shake her grass skirt like only Ms. Matheson could.

Then she said, "Here, let's play catch. Can you catch this ball?"

I caught it and threw it back. I put it kind of high so she had to jump way up for it. She caught it and landed with a jiggle. I climbed up onto the table, grabbed the beach ball out of her hands, and threw it over my shoulder. Then I took Ms. Matheson in my arms like I had always dreamed and pulled her close.

She smiled and said, "What about the ball?"

I tried to kiss her, but I heard her saying this over and over again.

"What about the ball? What about the ball?"

Her voice jolted me out of my reverie and back to reality.

"Huh?" I flinched in my seat. The students sitting at my table snickered.

"The ball. What about the ball? You didn't draw it. You have to include all the elements of the scene to get full credit for the project, Chris." Ms. Matheson said it quietly so the entire class did not hear her. She sensed I was a million miles away and she did not want to embarrass me too badly.

"Oh, yeah...the ball...sure," I said.

"Maybe you need a break, Chris. Would you run an errand for me? There are a few art supplies that were supposed to be delivered today. Would you please go to the Main Office and ask Mrs. Ryan if they came in?"

"Anything for you, Ms. Matheson," I said with a smile. I knew deep down she wanted me. It did not really matter; I had Elizabeth Allen to worry about back in the real world. As I headed down the hallway, I walked by Mr. Bulbsey's chemistry class where I saw Porter and Charles listening to one of his boring lectures. I gave a small wave to them as I passed by. If I had known what was going on in there I would have stayed a bit longer to eavesdrop.

"What do you mean it's wrong, Mr. Porter?" Bulbsey shouted. He pushed his glasses up off of the end of his nose. He was wearing his brown bombers that day. They were hiked way up over his belly button as usual.

"Your equation is incorrect," Porter said.

"How can it be incorrect?"

"When an equation doesn't have the right answer, then we use the word 'incorrect' to describe it." Charles sank down into his desk. This was not the first time Porter had corrected Bulbsey. He had a knack for knocking teachers off their mountains of educational superiority and pulling them down into the valleys where the rest of us commonfolk live.

"I've been teaching this class longer than you've been on this planet and you mean to tell me I don't know how to construct a simple chemical equation?"

"No. I'm saying you don't know how to do this particular one."

"You've got a lot of nerve, Mister! Don't you think after teaching this class for twenty-five years, I'd know what I'm doing?"

"You'd think." Bulbsey took a deep breath.

"Not only have I taught here at Wilson High for twenty-five years, but I also teach chemistry seminars at several area colleges. Do you think I could be as successful as I am if I were incompetent?" Bulbsey's face was getting red.

"You don't think you can make a mistake?" Porter asked.

"A mistake? I don't think so."

"The answer is seven point two five."

"Seven point two five? That's not even close to what I have. Are you saying you can look at this complicated twelve-step scientific equation and just come up with seven point two five in your head?"

"I'm saying maybe you don't understand the physical properties of H_2O."

"Water? What does water have to do with this problem, Mr. Porter?"

"It doesn't have anything to do with this problem. I just don't think you fully understand the properties of water. Otherwise, you'd know that Jesus Christ was the only person in world history who was perfect enough to walk on it. Your pompous ass would just sink."

The entire class gasped. Charles buried his face in his notebook. A few classmates tried to hide their chuckling and giggling. Proving Mr. Bulbsey was not perfect in front of the entire class was very dangerous territory.

"Get out! Get out of my classroom, Mr. Porter! Report to the Principal's Office immediately!" Bulbsey turned his back on the class. Porter grabbed his things, stood up, and began to leave the room. As he approached the door, he grabbed the chalk off of the chalk tray and fixed the problem.

"You forgot to carry a one here. When you make even the slightest error in the beginning of a problem it can drastically affect the final outcome. But you don't need me to tell you because you already knew that." Porter flipped the chalk onto the tray, winked at Charles, and exited the room the way a cowboy would leave a saloon after gunning down a bad guy. You could almost see the doors swinging back and forth behind him.

As he walked down the hallway, Porter went by Nick's history class so he appropriately yelled, "Woodcock!" as he passed. Mr. Woodcock ran to see who it was, but Porter turned the corner just as Woodcock made it to the door. He bit his lip to keep from saying something inappropriate. After a deep breath, Mr. Woodcock returned to his class.

"Now class, where were we? Oh yes, Mohandas Gandhi and the concept of passive resistance. You see, people called Mohandas Gandhi 'Mahatma' because the term means 'a person to be revered for high-mindedness, wisdom, and selflessness.'" Woodcock grabbed the eraser and put it to work. Unfortunately for him, one of his clever students had placed a piece of chalk in the eraser and it made a big mess when he went to erase the board. The class tried to muffle their laughter. This was not the first prank pulled on Woodcock. The students loved to get after him. Maybe it was because he always handled it so poorly.

"Ha...Ha...Very funny. That's a good freshman joke. As they say, simple pleasures for simple minds," he said. "Now as I was saying, Gandhi preached a technique called passive resistance..." Before he could finish writing those two words on the board a huge spitball smacked against the black slate right next to his furious hand. "All right, who threw that? Who threw it? You folks think you're really funny, don't you? Was it you, Mr. Barnard?

What are you snickering at Ms. Buduson? Believe me, you will get yours." His lips quivered with the agony of defeat as he scraped the sloppy, wet carcass off of the board and deposited it in the trash can.

"Now then, as I was saying, passive resistance is the concept that no matter how violent or intimidating a group of oppressors can be, the victim does not retaliate with violence." As he finished this statement he went over to sit down at his desk without seeing the whoopee cushion Nick had planted on his chair right before class. That's right—the infamous fart noise that has been a crowd-pleaser in high schools for countless years.

This time the students who had been trying to keep quiet all period howled in laughter. Nick was famous for this, but teachers could never prove he did it so he often got off without any punishment. Woodcock's entire body slouched and his head fell down onto his desk. "Mr. Armstrong? Could you please place this in the trash receptacle?"

"It isn't mine, Mr. Woodcock, you didn't see me put it there, did you?"

"I'm sure it isn't yours, Mr. Armstrong. I would never think a football player would do anything so juvenile, especially since you focus so much time on push-ups instead of academics." The students winced at the blatant insult. At this point, Woodcock did not care who the culprit was; he just wanted to unleash his venom on someone. Nick was one of his favorite targets.

Nick walked over, took the cushion out of Woodcock's hand, and dropped it into the trash can. Then he did something he knew he should not have, but when you are the starting quarterback you have to save face in honor of the rest of the team. He went back to his seat and politely raised his hand.

"Mr. Armstrong? Do you have a question?" Woodcock asked.

"Yeah, I was just wonderin' about the times when Gandhi did all that fasting."

"Yes, he fasted to focus media attention on India's plight of injustice. The government was afraid of the public's reaction if Gandhi died. They didn't want his blood on their hands. This was a great example of passive resistance. Did you have a specific question about that?"

"I was just wonderin' how much Gandhi weighed. I remember seein' pictures of him and he couldn't have weighed more than a hundred pounds."

"Yes, Mr. Armstrong, he lost a significant amount of weight to prove his dedication to his cause. He fasted for days, weeks, and even months at a time. He lost so much weight some say he more closely resembled a corpse than a living, human body."

Just then Nick mumbled under his breath, "I bet he could still kick your sissy ass." The class erupted.

"What was that? What did you say? Did you have something else to add, Mr. Armstrong?" Woodcock glared at him.

"No, sir. I didn't say anything."

"Well then...let's get back to work. About ten years ago..."

"You bought your underwear and you've worn them every day since," Nick mumbled once again. This time Woodcock was onto him. After the chorus of giggles subsided, Woodcock turned around with daggers in his eyes.

Without a single gesture, Woodcock said, "To the Office, Mr. Armstrong. I'm going to make you regret this...and, boy, I mean it."

"What'd I do? Ah, man. Okay. Okay." Nick knew he was out of line, but it was difficult not to be at times with Mr. Woodcock. So he grabbed his things and marched down to the Principal's Office.

When Nick arrived, Porter and I had already gone over the "Bulbsey Incident" in full detail. I could not wait to hear Charles's reaction to it. Nick walked up to the door and paused as he spotted us through the window. Then he slowly dragged himself in.

"Well, look who's here," I smiled. "What happened to you?"

"That damn Woodcock got me. He made me so mad I called him a sissy and I said somethin' about Gandhi kickin' his ass and how he wore old underwear and he must've heard me."

"You gotta be kiddin' me? You let that weasel get to you?" Porter said.

"He insulted me because I'm a jock and he accused me of puttin' a whoopee cushion on his chair."

"Well...did ya?" I asked.

"Of course I did, but he didn't know that. Besides he's got no right talkin' down to me. When I graduate I swear I'm gonna come back here and kick his ass."

"Calm down. You're just all pissed off because ya know that Old Man Crutcher is gonna come down hard on ya," Porter said and winked at me. "Old Man Crutcher" is our affectionate name for our principal. He was tough and just a look from him would scare you. I was glad I was not waiting in line to see him.

"What are you two doin' here?" Nick asked.

"I'm just waitin' for Mrs. Ryan to see if any art supplies came in for Ms. Matheson."

"You suck up. What about you, Sherlock?"

"I got into it with Bulbsey again."

"No way! That's the third time this month."

"It was funny though, Nick. You gotta hear the story," I said.

"Yeah, but didn't Old Man Crutcher say he was gonna call your dad next time this happened?" Nick asked.

"Yeah. He did," Porter said. The three of us sat there in silence. Porter's old man was nobody you wanted to deliver bad news to. Porter never talked about him. Few of us had even seen him, but we knew he was a tough old son of a gun. My mom heard stories from the other mothers in the neighborhood and they did not sound too good.

"Well, it looks like Mrs. Ryan is comin' back with the art supplies. I guess I'll have to deliver these to my princess and gain a few more brownie points. I'm way ahead of all you guys now. I may have to actually contemplate goin' to the dance with her. Let's see, Ms. Matheson or Elizabeth Allen? Ms. Matheson or Elizabeth Allen? These are the times that try men's souls, gentlemen."

"We know. We know. Everything's goin' your way right now. Don't gloat. You never know when your Irish luck is gonna run out," Porter said. I politely took the supplies from Mrs. Ryan. All the secretaries in the school loved me because Charles and Mary had established our family's good reputation.

Just when I thought I was going back to my lovely one in art class, something happened, the significance of which cannot be understated. My father used to tell me that most people do not recognize the most significant moments in their life until they look back on them years later. I did not need the passage of time for further enlightenment. I knew immediately that this one was a doozy.

I threw Porter and Nick a "so long suckers" and began backing out of the office when I noticed someone standing behind me, holding the door open. As I turned to see who it was, there stood a scrawny, gawky, clumsy girl struggling to keep the heavy door from knocking her over. It was Kimmie Fitzgerald. She was this sad, little shadow of a girl everyone made fun of at Wilson High.

Kimmie walked around school all day with the proverbial "kick me" sign on her back. She wore her hair in pigtails, which all the girls abandoned in grade school, and socks pulled up to her knees. To make matters worse, she wore glasses. Half of the student body called her "four eyes" right to her face. Kimmie was used to such abuse and pretended it did not bother her. I knew better.

I realized even when I was a young kid that there was a tortured soul under that façade she used to shield her feelings. I did not even mention she had what people back then called a "hare lip." Her upper lip was slightly deformed at birth and it obviously wreaked havoc on her social life. Kimmie and I grew up together. I always tried to be nice to her. Kids called her names and made her the victim of countless practical jokes. There was always room to make fun of poor Kimmie. One time, I am ashamed to say, I even joined in.

Back in third grade my gym class was engrossed in a game of kickball. It was one of my favorites as a kid. Kimmie came up to the plate and everyone was saying she was an easy out. I was pitching well and getting everybody out. My confidence soared to the point where I was getting a little too cocky for my own good. I really wanted to win the game, but I also wanted to seem cool in front of the other kids. I was just starting to become close with Nick and Goodie.

Well, anyway, Kimmie kicked the ball right back to me. It slowly bounced into my hands. All her teammates were yelling, "Run, Kimmie, run!" I grabbed the ball and purposely held onto it for a few seconds. I thought it would be really dramatic and kind of funny if I let her think she had a chance to make it and then I would hit her right before she got to the base. Well, all my teammates shouted for me to throw the ball, but I waited. I smiled and let her get closer and closer to the base. All the kids were screaming on both sides of the field. Kimmie's eyes widened as she closed in on the base. She gave it everything she had. She honestly thought she would make it. It would be the first time she got to first base.

Kimmie was four steps away...three...two. At that moment I wound up and threw the ball as hard as I could...right at her head. I do not know why I did it. I guess I thought the suspense of her being so close to success and then tasting defeat would show the class some drama and comedy as well. All I remember was her hitting the ground and then the teacher running over to her. The kids gathered around her for what felt like an eternity. No one moved, particularly not Kimmie. She was out cold.

My mother talked to the teacher on the phone and said I would be punished for my actions and I needed to learn a lesson. I played it over and over in my mind for days. For the first time in my life I felt true regret. I sat in my room, crying and crying. I felt so ashamed. I could not believe I joined the crowd of all the other mean kids who tormented this helpless girl. To this day I still have not forgotten how mean that was. I will never forget.

I was finally able to show my face in the neighborhood after I suffered two weeks of menial labor around the house. Mom made me apologize to Kimmie and then walk her to school every single day for the rest of the school year. Her plan worked because Kimmie and me became quite close after spending all that time together. I got to know her as a person with feelings, interests, and dreams. By the time we made it to high school, I considered her a friend. Of course, I would not want too many people to know that. I mean, I usually dodged her in the halls when I was with my friends at school. Then I usually felt guilty so I would spend some time with her around the neighborhood.

"Hey, Chris! Let me hold the door for you. Where are you goin' with all that?"

"Hi, Kimmie. I'm just bringin' it to Ms. Matheson's class."

"I've been lookin' for you around the neighborhood for the past few days. I've been meanin' to ask you...um...do you know about...um...the Homecoming Dance...next week?"

"Yeah. I'm lookin' forward to it," I said.

"Oh, so...you already...have a date?"

"Well...not exactly. Why?" I stopped and stared at her as I cleared the doorway. Nick and Porter listened as she continued to hold the door.

"I just wanted to know...if you'd...go with me?" Her eyes stared at me the same way they did that sunny day back in third grade.

I looked at the guys with panic and struggled to think of something. What could I say? I could not possibly go with Kimmie. What about Elizabeth? If she asked me, I could not blow an opportunity like that. Besides, how could I ever explain going with Kimmie? She would ruin my image for sure. All the guys would make fun of me. A million thoughts flew by like trees passing a car, speeding down a highway.

"I...uh...that would be great...uh...but...I...uh...I already have a date." The words came out of my mouth uncontrollably. I could not believe it. I almost came clean and said I was just joking and I would go with her, but I paused just long enough for her to escape the awkward situation.

As she let go of the door and started walking away she said over her shoulder, "Oh, you do...well, that's okay...maybe next time. Besides, there are a couple of other guys I could go with too." I watched her walk down the hallway, hanging her head. I knew no one else would go with her. It was awful. Just that morning I woke up with aspirations of entering into Wilson High immortality. If I went with Elizabeth we could dance and kiss all night, but I knew that after talking to Kimmie I would be consumed, thinking about poor, little Kimmie Fitzgerald sitting home playing board games with her parents.

Nick and Porter glanced at me for a moment and then looked away. What had I done? It all happened so quickly. As I watched Kimmie walk down the hallway the sun came through the windows and kissed the side of her face. In my head I could hear the kids cheering as I released the kickball from my hand. I knocked her out cold again. This time, I was not sure she would get back up.

TEN

"To thine own self be true."

WILLIAM SHAKESPEARE

Wilson High was not the most aesthetically pleasing school in Upstate New York. Although it looked like a classic school building comprised of bricks and concrete on the outside, its dominant interior colors were gray and light blue. The floors were made up of tiles with gray and white flecks and the walls were predominantly a faded pale blue. However, the building has always had a couple of nice features. There were two parallel breezeways on the main floor that connected the two central parts of the school. In one part there were classrooms and the library. The other part, which was connected by the breezeways, housed the offices, cafeteria, gymnasium, and auditorium.

The breezeways were basically two long hallways with all glass windows on either side. When the weather was nice the custodians would open the windows and an invigorating breeze would sweep across the courtyard between them. Every year in May, they landscaped the courtyard to make it into a pleasant, little park in the middle of the premises. They planted flowers and brought out benches and tables so people could eat lunch outside. It remained like that until late fall when the weather started to get too cold.

The only downside was there was virtually no privacy at all. On one side, you had your friends waving to you out of the classroom windows. On the opposite side, you had the Main Office which was always well-manned. And the other two sides of the courtyard were the two long, glass corridors where people were constantly walking by. It definitely favored the exhibitionist over the recluse.

I almost forgot to mention the courtyard's greatest feature—a pond was put in last summer by a few skilled landscapers. That's right, Mr. Nick Armstrong and his faithful sidekick, Sebastian Goodsen. Old Man Crutcher heard Nick put a pond in his parents' backyard and he knew he would work cheap. One day he traveled over to the Armstrong's house to see it. He was so impressed he told Nick the school would hire him to do it for ten dollars. That was a whole summer's worth of peddlin' newspapers.

Nick and Goodie did a great job. It had rocks all around it and lily pads floating in the water around a spectacular fountain that shot water up in the middle. Goodie planted some beautiful flowers and stocked it up with goldfish. It was the talk of the town. Families came from all over town to see it. Nick and Goodie got their picture in the newspaper with Old Man Crutcher. It hangs from the mirror in my room.

It was around eleven thirty when I passed down the glass corridor on my way to the cafeteria for lunch. I had not seen Elizabeth all morning. I heard through the grapevine that she and Deke had gotten into a shouting match second period in front of Ms. Button's room. I did not really know what it could have been about because, according to reports, they had already broken up.

After devouring my turkey sandwich and potato chips I walked over to the breezeway to see if I could spot Elizabeth. She was heading right toward me with my cousin, Anna, by her side. She was wearing a beautiful pink dress and a bright smile. Our eyes met and I forgot all my troubles. The big moment had arrived.

"Hey, Chris! I've been lookin' for you all day," Elizabeth shouted down the hall.

"Yeah? I thought maybe you were tryin' to avoid me. Hey, Anna, what's goin' on?" My nervous hands went right into my pockets.

Anna gave me a funny smirk. Elizabeth turned to her and said, "Anna, I need to talk to Chris for a minute. You go ahead. I'll catch up." Then Elizabeth turned to me and nodded her head as if she wanted me to follow her.

"What's the deal, Elizabeth?" I loved being close enough to smell her hair.

"Come outside into the courtyard. It's such a lovely day and I want a minute alone with you."

"Are you sure you just want a minute? Honey, you can take all day if you'd like." Suddenly, I felt this overwhelming reassurance. I loosened up and took my hands out of my pockets.

71

"Well, I wanna tell you I had a great time the other night and I've been thinkin' about you," she said as she walked me over to a shaded bench by a maple tree.

"I'm glad to hear that," I said, using my best baritone voice. I slowly reached out and took her hand in mine. "I wanna let you know I had a great time too. I think you're the prettiest girl around and I was honored to have been worthy enough to spend time alone with you."

"Get outta here! You don't have to feel worthy. I'm a regular girl just like anyone else in this school. I mean...I suppose I'm prettier and cooler than most, but I guess, deep down, we're all kinda similar, except for the real losers, of course."

"Yeah...I guess." My eyes wandered over to the breezeway and I noticed Charles walking out of the cafeteria with Nick, Porter, and Goodie. They spotted me and gave a few sarcastic waves. I let go of Elizabeth's hand. I wondered if Charles knew about what I did to Kimmie.

"Are you listenin' to me?"

"Huh? Oh...I'm sorry. I guess I drifted off for a second. What were you sayin'?" I asked.

"You might wanna pay attention to this. I don't wanna have to say it twice."

"I'm sorry, go ahead."

"I was saying...the Homecoming Dance is coming up next weekend and out of all the boys who wanna go with me this year, I've decided you would be the best date for me."

If I accepted, people would look at me differently from all different corners of the school. I looked at her perfectly-manicured fingernails. I took in her flawless make-up that needlessly tried to enhance her beauty. I admired her cute, little purse that stylishly matched her outfit. She looked perfect, almost too perfect. She seemed unreal.

"I'd love to take you to the dance," I said. I did it! It was official. I was going to the Homecoming Dance with Elizabeth Allen. No one would ever be able to take that away from me. I was in a whole new class of people at Wilson High.

"Spectacular! The first thing we need to do is buy you some clothes. I just purchased a new dress and, of course, you'll need to match my color scheme. And then there's the car situation. I told all my friends about your uncle's magnificent car so you have to tell him you need to borrow it. I know you can't legally drive so Hannah's boyfriend will have to."

"What? Drive my uncle's car? Who's Hannah's boyfriend?"

"Then we'll have to make reservations at the Brooke House Restaurant for before the dance. It's the most happening place in town. All the sophisticated people dine there. I hope you've been saving your money. It's very expensive and you have to pay for the two of us."

"The Brooke House? Sure, I've been savin' my money, but..." As my ears started to tune her out I noticed a dozen of her girlfriends had suddenly closed in on us for all the details.

"We're on for the dance. And he's gonna get his uncle's car too!" Elizabeth shouted to her gal pals who shrieked with excitement. Something did not feel right. I could hear my brother's voice over and over saying, "I just can't seem to like that Elizabeth Allen very much." Charles and the rest of my buddies were watching from the breezeway. Unlike Elizabeth's friends, they did not come running over to congratulate me. What happened? One minute I was enjoying a quiet moment alone with a beautiful girl and the next I felt lost in a crowd. I had no control over what was going on.

"Hey, Elizabeth, can your man here hold his liquor?" Hannah asked.

"Are you kiddin'? He can drink all of you under the table. Besides, my man and me are gonna do a lot more than just drink. Isn't that right, cutie pie?" They all cheered her on.

More than just drink? Cutie pie? I was so embarrassed I just smiled and nodded in agreement. I could see Charles frowning across the way.

Then a cheerleader named Grace popped in, "Hey, Elizabeth, are you sure this young freshman knows what he's gettin' himself into? Can he really handle a girl like you?"

"Of course he can. If he really behaves himself I may even have to take him to a private location at Murphy's, if you know what I mean." She wrapped her arms around my waist. They were talking about me as if I were not even there. She was calling all the shots, making all the decisions, and giving me all the orders.

I looked all around for Anna. I thought maybe she could get me out of this, but she disappeared. This was not exactly her crowd. These girls were trouble. I needed to put a stop to it, but I did not know how. Everything was moving too fast. I looked over to see if I could give a signal to Charles, but he was not looking my way. Then something happened that I know was a sign from above. Out of the corner of my eye I saw someone walk over and sit down all alone at a table in the far corner of the courtyard. It was Kimmie.

"Look who's here. It's Supernerd," one of the girls said. All of them pointed and laughed. Kimmie ignored them as best she could. She pulled out a sandwich and an apple and began eating without raising her head. She had learned that if she did not make eye contact they would eventually leave her alone.

"Who d'ya think she'll be takin' to the dance?" someone asked.

"Probably her dad!" Elizabeth said. "What d'ya think, Chris? Maybe we could double."

I could see that kickball raised high and aimed right at little Kimmie again. I prayed I could find a way out of this horrible situation. And then I heard a voice in my head tell me what to do and it seemed so simple. I took the kickball in my hand, turned around, and fired it.

"I have to be honest, Elizabeth. I think I'd be embarrassed," I said.

"Of course you would. Don't worry. I'd never let us be seen with a loser like that."

"No, I mean, I'd be embarrassed to have everyone see me with a piece of trash like you." The kickball smashed against Elizabeth's phony face.

"What? Are you kiddin'?"

"No. I'm not. You all think you're so cool and perfect. Well, you're not. I have way too much pride to lower myself to your standards. I would never talk about another person like that. And besides, Kimmie is a friend of mine."

"Well, then why don't you go take her to the dance and join the 'loser-of-the-month' club?"

"Ya know what? That's not a bad idea. By the way, 'Liz,' you really are a beautiful girl...on the outside. But my father once told me beauty is only skin deep. If that's the case, you got a whole lotta ugly inside of you. In fact, I'd say someone beat the hell outta ya with the ugly stick." Elizabeth just stood there with her mouth open. No one ever talked to her like that before. Even her friends stood paralyzed in absolute disbelief.

"Well, I don't have to stand here and take this. Who do you think you are? You must be out of your mind to turn down a date with me. C'mon girls, let's get outta here!" she said through clenched teeth.

"But, Elizabeth, what about the car? You said he was gonna get us his uncle's cool car, didn't you?" Ellie asked.

"Just shut up! Everybody leave me alone!" Elizabeth shouted as she pushed her way through the crowd. Then I walked over to Kimmie's table.

"Kimmie?"

"Hey, Chris."

"Is that invitation to the dance still open?"

"Of course it is."

"Well, I'd like to take you up on it...if you still wanna go with me."

"I'd love to, Chris. That would be great! We'll have a terrific time together. Don't you think we will?"

"I *know* we will."

"I'm so excited. I have to go get a dress!" she said as she packed up what was left of her lunch.

"C'mon, let's go back inside. The bell's gonna ring any second," I said as I grabbed her books and walked her toward the breezeway. As we passed through the door I noticed Charles and the boys standing in the hall just smilin' at me. They saw the whole thing. When I walked past my brother he gave me a huge pat on the back. I felt redeemed. It was the right thing to do and I did it all on my own. Charles did not have to come bail me out like he always did.

Elizabeth Allen left the courtyard, swearing like a sailor while her friends tried to figure out what had just happened. I hit her with that kickball right between the eyes. She never saw it coming. The game was over. For the first time, Kimmie stood in the winner's circle.

I knew Charles did not want me to go with that fool, Elizabeth. I should have trusted his instincts instead of listening to my hormones. As I walked Kimmie to her locker, the boys all walked by me and put in their two cents.

"You did the right thing, Chris," Charles said as he passed by me.

"Well, sir, I've always admired you for your integrity and this is just another reason why," Goodie said as he shook my hand. He and Charles exited to the right.

Then Porter whispered in my ear, "Hey, great job, goin' with the Fitzgerald girl, huh? I hear she puts out."

Nick could not resist joining in the ribbing, "Maybe if you're lucky she'll let you take her into the back room at Murphy's?" he said and then joined Porter as they exited to the left. I suppose I deserved it since I had been acting so high-and-mighty.

I dropped Kimmie off at her locker, which was aptly chosen for her right next to the restroom. We got our locker assignments in the beginning of the year and it looked like Kimmie was last in line.

"All right, Kimmie. I'll call you later tonight and we'll work out some of the arrangements, okay?"

"Great. Do you still have my number?"

"Yeah. I think my mom has it written down somewhere."

"Thanks again, Chris. I can't wait." She gave me a big hug. I walked away and headed up the stairs to get to my locker before I was late to my next class.

By the end of the day I had a pretty good idea that news of my "Elizabeth Allen bashing" had spread. As I walked down the hall I noticed different groups of people seemed to be staring at me. One pair of girls even pointed and giggled as I passed by. I prayed the news did not travel that fast. Maybe I was just being paranoid. Then I turned down the hall to go to my locker and I cut through a group of five cheerleaders.

I heard one of them say, "That's the little runt who dumped on Elizabeth. I guess he wants to spend the rest of his high school years as an outcast." I tried to ignore them and keep walking, but I could not help but look back. Their stares were sharp knives that pierced my thin skin. I knew I had to get out of there as fast as I could. I needed to dart to my locker, grab my belongings, and get home.

As I approached my locker, I noticed there was a group of football players gathered around it. They were not the players Nick usually hung out with. These were the guys none of us liked very much. They thought they were really cool because they dated all of the cheerleaders. I recognized them instantly from their blue and white letterman jackets. I calmly said, "Excuse me, guys. Can I get through? You're in front of my locker."

They turned and sized me up and then dispersed. As their bodies parted I saw over one guy's shoulder there was something written in red on my locker. Another guy crossed in front, obstructing my view. What was it? I could not see it clearly. They finally moved and I stood with an unobstructed view. I was face to face with the word "LOSER" written in red lipstick across the locker door. I stood there in terror. Everyone seemed to be staring and laughing at me. Everything was moving in slow-motion. I labored over my locker combination. Thirty-one, twenty, twenty-three? Twenty-three, twenty, thirty-one? Twenty, twenty-three, thirty-one? I could not stand it. I abandoned all my things and ran down the hall and out the door. I did not stop running until I got home. I could not wait for Charles or the other guys. I just wanted to hide. I wanted to run up into my room and bury my head under my pillow.

I knew I should not have lost my temper. I knew I should have stayed with Elizabeth. If I went to that dance with Kimmie, I would never be able to show my face in school again. I was just starting to become somebody and then everything seemed to be falling apart. I knew after that fateful day that they would never think I was cool...never.

ELEVEN

"It is a rough road that leads to the heights of greatness."

SENECA

I sat at the dinner table, staring at my food. I had never noticed all the intricate details of mashed potatoes. Mom made them so light and fluffy. My mind wandered and they suddenly became different cloud formations. The first dollop on the plate—a cumulus. The fork cut across it—a cirrus, and so on.

I wanted to be up in a cloud so I could get away from everyone and everything. I was so upset about what happened and so consumed with worry about the dance. I could not think of anything else.

"They're fascinating aren't they?" Dad asked.

"Huh?"

"Mashed potatoes. They're fascinating. I remember when you and your brother could play with mashed potatoes for hours. Of course, that was about ten years ago. I've grown accustomed to seeing you eat them."

"Is something wrong, Chris? You seem awfully distracted tonight?" Mom asked.

"No. Nothin's wrong. I just don't feel like talkin'."

"Why don't you just tell 'em," Charles said.

"Tell us what?"

"Nothing! I don't wanna talk about it, okay?" I paused for a moment and then felt foolish for snapping at my mother so I quickly asked if I could be excused from the table. My father gave me a nod so I high-tailed it up to my room and buried my head in my pillow.

The first thing on my mind was I could not get over the pity I felt for poor Kimmie. She was helpless. Kids picked on her all the time and I knew things would only get worse at the dance. Kimmie was not the only thing on my mind though. I was also feeling personally cheated by the whole situation. I had come so far. I wanted desperately to fit in during my freshman year of high school and I had blown it. I thought I could date the prettiest girl in school, have plenty of friends, get good grades, and succeed at sports. Who was I kidding? How could a kid be popular who did not drink, smoke, and take pretty girls into the back room at Murphy's parties?

There was a knock at the door. "Come in."

"Okay, let's talk," Mom said. "Charles said some kids pulled a mean prank on you at school. D'ya wanna tell me about it?" She sat down on the bed next to me.

"I don't know. I thought I did the right thing, but it feels wrong already."

"What'd you do?"

"I got asked to the Homecoming Dance by Kimmie from across the street. Ya know, it's a turnaround dance, so the girls ask the guys?"

"Right, the girls ask the guys. I've been listening to your sister go on and on about it all week. So, did you tell Kimmie you could go?"

"At first I didn't because I wanted to go with this other girl."

"Who?"

"Elizabeth Allen."

"Elizabeth Allen? Isn't she that cheerleader who hangs out with Anna? Ya know, your aunt and uncle aren't too impressed with her. They don't really like Anna spending time with her...something about some tough boys that are her friends or something."

"Yeah, but she's really pretty and she likes me or at least I thought she did. Well, anyway. I told Kimmie I couldn't go with her and then Elizabeth asked me and I said I would."

"Sounds like you got what you wanted, so what's the problem?"

"Elizabeth started bossing me around in front of all her friends. She told everybody that I would get Uncle Bobby's car to drive to the dance."

"What? Doesn't sound like the kind of girl you'd like to bring home to meet your father and me, does it?"

"Not at all! And then she went on to make fun of poor Kimmie right in front of her."

"I think I know where this is headed. I hope you did the right thing."

"Don't worry, Mom. I did. I told Elizabeth I wouldn't go with her, in so many words, and then I asked Kimmie if she still wanted to go with me."

"That was a very kind and considerate gesture, Chris. I'm very proud of you. That Elizabeth Allen should be ashamed of herself, acting like that. You take Kimmie and have fun."

"But that's the thing. Everyone's gonna make fun of me. They wrote 'LOSER' on my locker in bright-red lipstick. I can't take Kimmie now. If I do, I'll never be able to show my face in school again." Mom gently put her hand on my back.

"Now, Christopher. What have your father and I taught you? You have to think of others ahead of yourself, especially with someone like poor Kimmie. She doesn't have anyone out there standing up for her, but you became that someone. You took a very difficult stand. You see, I know being popular is important in high school. But don't forget...being honorable is important your entire life.

"You did the honorable thing by standing up for Kimmie. It'll pay off in the end. You see, God gives people certain challenges to see how they'll handle them. Some people run from challenges and take the easy way out. Others decide to meet those challenges. It's those people who practice true faith in themselves and God. Now let me ask you this...do you honestly think you should have gone with Elizabeth instead of Kimmie?"

"No, of course not."

"Then you know, deep down, you did the right thing. Your heart pointed you in the right direction. It's the next step that's difficult. Now you have to carry the plan through. You're right, it may not be easy, but it'll be worth it in the end.

"Any young, arrogant fool can walk into the Homecoming Dance with the prettiest girl on his arm, but it takes a true gentleman of integrity to walk in with someone others ridicule. You're making a statement to everyone there that Kimmie is a beautiful person and she demands respect and I believe you'll help her get it. Kimmie is a great person and she deserves to be treated like a princess for at least one night. Don't you think so? You're just as lucky to be going with her as she is to be going with you.

"You know what I think? I think you'll be surprised at how many kids won't pick on you or Kimmie at all. If anything, they'll admire you for standing up for your beliefs. It's not an easy thing to stand alone and face the criticism of your peers." Mom always made a lot of sense. She could convince me of anything.

She continued, "Furthermore, you may open up Kimmie's world to a whole new group of people. I don't understand why you keep talking about being popular. You have plenty of friends. For all you know, this is God's way of giving you an opportunity to help this girl meet some new people. Who knows, you may even end up meeting someone special yourself."

"I know you're right, Mom. Thanks for talkin' me through this."

"I'll call the school and make sure they get a custodian to clean up your locker. Now that doesn't mean all the harsh words are over. You may still have to face those who are insecure and think they need to pick on you to feel big. If that happens just remember they're the ones you should feel sorry for, not Kimmie. I'm sure Kimmie is thrilled to be going with you so stop thinking so much about yourself and put her needs first. Don't let her down. Show her you're proud to call her your date and make sure she has fun. You owe her that much."

"Thanks, Mom. You and Dad are always there for me and I really appreciate it. I love you very much," I said as I gave her a warm hug.

"I love you too. Now go finish your dinner and expect at least one cruel joke from your father. That's just his way of showing you he loves you."

As I walked back into the dining room and sat down, they had already moved on to dessert. I knew Charles told them the whole story so it was out in the open.

Dad started in on me, "Well, Chris, it's not gonna be easy bein' the father of the most unpopular kid in school. It sure ain't gonna be a walk in the park. I guess we'll have more time to spend together on the weekends seein' as you won't be goin' out very much."

"Yeah and you can play Yahtzee with Mom and Dad on Saturday nights while Charles and me go out and have a life." Mary was so much like my dad it was uncanny.

My locker was cleaned up the next day. I focused on Mom's advice and ignored the staring and pointing from all of the gossips.

As the week carried on, it got easier to deal with and eventually it all seemed to settle down. Charles and the rest of the fellas made it easy. They knew it was a tough time for me, but they stood by me like the true friends they were. My dad wrote a saying on my notebook some guy named Thucydides once said. It read, "We secure our friends not by accepting favors, but by doing them." My friends were showing me a sign of loyalty I would never forget.

The night of the Homecoming Dance had arrived. This was my first high school dance and I wanted to look my best. I shared bathroom and mirror time with Charles and Mary. Charles gave me some clothing advice and Dad helped me make a Double Windsor knot in my tie. Mary and her closest friends went with some of the football players.

In typical Charles's fashion, he convinced Anna to double with Kimmie and me. He always looked out for his baby brother. My uncle let him drive the '57 Chevy Corvette. I had to pretend it was a huge honor riding in it because it was supposed to be my first time. Jack lost out to Anna because he was younger so he got stuck driving my aunt's Edsel—it wasn't pretty.

After my uncle gave Charles the lecture about being responsible with the car, we went to pick up Kimmie. She lived around the corner from us so Charles drove the Corvette down our street to show it off in front of our neighbors. I have to admit I felt pretty cool just being a passenger. Elizabeth Allen sure was missing out. When we made it to Kimmie's house, Charles and Anna were kind enough to go in with me. After Charles straightened my tie, I took a deep breath and rang the doorbell. Kimmie's mom opened it before I even removed my finger from the button. I was nervous, but I knew I had to make sure Kimmie had a good time.

Kimmie's mom knew my family had a good reputation and she was obviously thrilled Kimmie was not going to be spending the evening up in her room. Mr. Fitzgerald is a very nice, quiet guy. He speaks very softly, but you can tell he means every word he says. He is honest and humble. I was calmed by the big smile he flashed me as he rose from the couch to meet us in the doorway.

Kimmie's mom called for her while we all stood in the living room. As I looked at the stairs leading up to the second flight, I saw a pair of scrawny legs slowly appear. Like a helpless deer, peeking out of the woods, Kimmie made her painful first appearance. To be honest, I thought she looked kind of cute.

She took time with every detail. She let her hair fall down over her shoulders which was a refreshing change of pace. She wore a touch of make-up too, no lipstick though. Our outfits went together quite well. I wore Navy blue pants with a white shirt and a blue tie. She picked out a Navy blue skirt with a white blouse. I was feeling better and better as the evening drew on. I quickly walked over to her with a big smile and complimented her politely on how nice she looked. She blushed.

Mrs. Fitzgerald made us pose for tons of pictures. Her father put a stop to it after awhile. I made sure I held the door open for Kimmie as we left. On the way out, her dad slipped me a few bucks "for an ice cream sundae after the dance." Charles and Anna were masters at making small talk and they quickly soothed Kimmie and me. They had a black and white theme going on. Like most of the girls at school, Anna wore a dress with polka dots. The black and white colors looked very sharp.

We were on our way. Charles took a few extra laps around the neighborhood before we went to the school. After all, it was only five minutes away and we wanted as many people as possible to see us driving around in that Corvette. The sun set just as we arrived. Many of the other students showed up before we did. I kept reflecting on all of my mom's advice. She had always been a source of great strength for me.

What truly bothered me the moment I stepped out of that magical '57 machine was many of our closest friends would not be with us. Nick was forced to sit it out. Mr. Woodcock met with his parents about the incident at school on Monday and part of his punishment was he was prohibited from going to the dance. The only good thing about it was it probably diffused a dozen catfights between girls at school who wanted to ask him.

Then there was Porter. For some reason, he stayed clear of all those functions. Someone would have asked him, but everyone knew he did not go to dances. We never knew why, but we thought it had something to do with his old man.

And the final member of the gang who would be staying home was Goodie. The girls at school thought Goodie was adorable. A couple of them asked him, but he shied away. He did not like dancing and being involved with a lot of people who were "trying to act cool." Anyway, we promised we would all meet at Yorkie's afterward.

Charles and I opened the car doors for our dates as our father instructed us to do. They each took us by the arm and we commenced our walk down the red carpet and into this fantasy palace. The Homecoming Committee decorated the entire gymnasium like the inside of a castle. After all, we were the Wilson High Knights.

It was quite impressive. As we approached the main entrance to the gym there were students on the other side who lowered a drawbridge to let us in. After we passed through, they raised it up again. Some people made stupid jokes about it, but I could tell most thought it was pretty cool. The committee put light blue carpet all along the main entrance of the gym to make it look like a mote we had to cross to get in and out.

What really gave the room ambience were these large cardboard towers in each corner. The drama department used them in their production of "Camelot." I soon forgot it was the place where the guys would sweat while working-out, trying to impress all the girls. They set up the far end of the gym with a large platform for the band. Over their heads were several balconies where dummies, dressed in armor, chaperoned the night's events.

The final touch was supplied by the art department. They made these ten-foot tall tapestries, depicting medieval scenes. There were beautiful princesses blushing at men of chivalry, valiant gentlemen dueling and jousting, and a king that kind of looked like Old Man Crutcher, sitting high on his throne. They were somewhat amateurish, but they completed the motif nicely.

Mary and her friends made it a point to stop over and say hello. She always looked out for her brothers whether or not she wanted to admit it. Jack and Drew had not shown up at that point. Jack always arrived late like a master of suspense. He wanted everyone asking for him and worrying that he would not come and then he would explode onto the dance floor and steal the show. He was a great dancer.

My mood was improving by the minute. Kimmie looked thrilled to be there with me. Charles and Anna were great company. I was determined not to let anyone bother me with rude comments. I was proud to be with Kimmie. I did not care what other people thought. I was going to show her a great time. I owed her that much for all we had been through in the past. It felt good being surrounded by people who cared about me. Because of them, I knew I would look back on that night with fond memories.

TWELVE

"Always bear in mind that your own resolution to succeed is more important than any other one thing."

ABRAHAM LINCOLN

Five blocks away from school, a young man sat on his back porch entranced by the natural surroundings of his backyard and all its wonderment. As the sun set, a cool breeze lightly rustled the leaves in the trees while birds and other small creatures joined in to create nature's symphony. This was as therapeutic for Goodie as listening to Beethoven's *Moonlight Sonata*. "The Good One" as we affectionately called him from time to time, sat with a simple pad and pencil and labored to capture this sublime moment.

He could take in a scene that was constantly evolving and somehow freeze all the most magical aspects into a single image that transcended the world around him. I could sit next to him for hours and when he was done I would look at his drawings and feel like asking, "Where did you see that?" I am an observant person, but Goodie's eyes could see God at work.

His mom yelled out the window, "Sebastian, fire up the grill for your father. He's gonna make Hoffmann hot dogs for supper, special just for you."

"Sure...in a second," he said without taking his eyes off of the scene.

"I thought I'd also make your favorite homemade macaroni and cheese and baked beans. How does that sound?"

"Sounds good, Mom."

He finished putting the final touches on the weeping willow tree that was gently swaying in the breeze. He felt content with the rays of sun shining through and then a family of birds at his father's birdhouse hypnotized him. Goodie's father was what you call a lifelong learner. I never saw him without a book or a manual of some sort in his hands.

One of his favorite hobbies was building birdhouses in his basement workshop. He modeled this particular one after his own house. The resemblance was uncanny. Every detail was exactly the same: the roof, the windows, the doors, the colors, and all the

86

dimensions were identical. Charles and I marveled at it when we were kids. We loved pointing out the corner bedroom, which was Goodie's, and pretending we were giants, coming to crush him.

Goodie appreciated this family of birds that showed up. He felt a certain kinship with them as if they were sent exclusively to him. They stayed for the next few minutes and occupied Goodie's mind. Spending time alone did not bother him. There was a certain part of Goodie that no one could ever touch. He kept to himself and found ways to enjoy his solitude.

"Hey, maybe after dinner we'll take your Grandma out for ice cream," his mom said from the kitchen.

"Sure," Goodie said as he brought the birds to life on his pad. He was shading in the wings of the smallest one. They were spread wide as it flew away from the corner bedroom of the house. Although it seemed young and fragile, Goodie knew it could fly for miles and miles. Its destiny was far beyond those walls.

"Sebastian, please get the grill started."

"Oh, sorry, Mom. I forgot. I'll do it right now." He set down his pad and pencil and walked over to the grill. As he picked up the book of matches he saw his father's radio sitting on the shelf of the porch. The local radio station was broadcasting live from the dance. He reached down and turned it on. The life of Rock 'N' Roll filled the air.

"Dom, dom, dom, dom...dombee doobee,
dom, dom, dom, dom, dom...dombee doobee,
dom, dom, dom, dom, dom...dombee doobee, dom,
wah, wah, wah, waahaa.
Well, I love, love you darlin'...come and go with me..."

That song always puts me in a good mood. The band was starting the evening off right. Of course, I knew we were going to have some rough spots throughout the evening. The first one occurred when five couples suddenly fled from the table where Kimmie and I sat down. I could not help but just sit there and clench my teeth. As we mingled with a group of friends, I noticed Elizabeth had entered the building.

She was a knockout as always. Her hair was done up to make her look more mature. It worked. Her make-up was perfect, her jewelry was elegant, and she wore this incredible red dress with black polka dots. All eyes were on her when she entered the room. I was one of the few people who understood how her physical beauty masked her wickedness underneath. And yet, part of me still desperately wanted to have her on my arm. Charles saw me staring at her so he stopped what he was doing and stood next to me.

"She's as fake as those diamond earrings she's wearin'," he said.

"Yeah...I know, but..."

"Don't worry, Chris. Give her twenty minutes. I guarantee she'll make a complete idiot of herself. Besides, she's already taken the first step in the wrong direction. Did ya see who she came with?"

"No, who'd she come with?"

"Take a look." As I turned my head I saw the biggest jerk in Wilson High walk through the door. That's right—Deke Marshall. Anna took me aside and explained what was going on. Their shouting match on Monday was quite revealing. Anna heard Elizabeth tell Deke she was going to use me to make him jealous. Not only that, but she was also going to use me so she could go to the dance in my uncle's car. Without realizing it, I ruined her entire plan and she had to go crawling back to him.

As a couple, they were a complete mess. They fought constantly. In fact, a couple of times Old Man Crutcher had to call their parents because they were screaming at each other in the hall. What a joke! I knew with each passing minute I was better off without her.

"Yeah, that's the prettiest girl in school for sure, of course, it would help her if she had brains and morals, but I guess I'm just being critical," Charles said.

"I gotcha...I gotcha," I said with a smile. Kimmie asked me to get her some punch. When I went to get it, Elizabeth and her cronies circled the bowl. I politely asked if they would move.

Deke started all the fun, "I thought the nerds had to drink from a separate bowl."

Elizabeth joined in, "Deke, I'm so glad I'm here with you. I'd hate to think what people would have said if I came with *that* loser! Besides, he would probably be too nervous to even go to Murphy's party later on. He's just a kid. You're a real man."

I did not want to give them the satisfaction of seeing me get upset. Unfortunately, my hands betrayed me as they always do. I was so tense I could not get the punch into the damn cup without spilling it. They stood there laughing at me. After fumbling with it for a few seconds I retreated to my table. Charles calmed me down. Just then the band took the music up a notch. Jerry Lee Lewis was one of the crowd favorites.

> *"Come on over baby, whole lotta shakin' goin' on,*
> *Yes, I said come on over baby; baby you can't go wrong,*
> *We ain't fakin', whole lotta shakin' goin' on."*

The girls went wild and pulled their dates onto the dance floor in the center of the gym. Anna immediately turned to Charles.

"C'mon, Charles. We gotta dance. I love this song."

"Anything you say."

"Ya wanna join 'em?" I asked Kimmie.

"You bet." This part might sound funny, but we all took our shoes off and left them underneath our table. Then we literally danced in our socks—it was a sock hop, after all. It was actually great fun. For some reason I think people felt a little less inhibited dancing in their socks. No one worried about looking too cool.

We all loved to dance. There was a time when Charles and I used to be shy. The girls had to drag us onto the dance floor, but we got over it. I think it just dawned on us one day that all the girls were always on the floor. If you wanted to be with the girls, you had better learn how to dance. We learned how to jitterbug from our parents. They owned the dance floor in their day. Mary volunteered for many painful hours of Charles and me stepping on her toes, but she was pretty good about it.

I showed Kimmie how to do it. First you need rhythm. Kimmie was moving her feet well, so she obviously had it. Then I took her by the hands and we rocked left...right...back...forward. I brought my left hand up and threw my arm over her head. Then we rocked and I spun her back through. At first, I was not sure if she would be able to catch on, but she did. I stayed with those basic moves for a while. Concentrating on the dance helped keep my mind off of all the trouble surrounding us.

Charles and Anna were at the next level. They were spinning each other left and right and switching positions. Charles loved to do the move where you hold hands with your partner and then turn to your side. Then you lift your right arm over your head until the girl's left hand is on your left shoulder. Then you let it slide down your left arm until it meets your hand. It looks real smooth and Charles and Anna had perfected it. They were really cute together. I think one of the reasons was because there was not any real dating pressure. I wish more people could take a page out of their book and just be themselves.

Suddenly, the dance floor was packed. Electric bodies bounced up and down and slid back and forth. There was still no sign of Jack and Drew. We started to hope nothing bad had happened to them. We could not have a dance without Jack and Drew. This Italian girl named Theresa asked Jack. She was a great dancer and probably the only girl in school who could keep up with him. As usual, Kathy asked Drew. He just could not refuse her.

Mary and her athletic friends were being thrown up in the air by their strong football player dates. Mary's date was able to pull off the move where he picked her up off of the ground and swung her feet to the left of his body, then to the right, and then all the way around his body and he caught her. It was amazing. My sister had a lot of style too. He could not have made it work without her. I was in the center of the dance floor, surrounded by a couple hundred people and I did not feel self-conscious at all. Kimmie and I were having fun and I kept telling myself that was all that mattered.

Six blocks away from school, a young man sat on his workout bench, taking a break from lifting weights. Poor Nick Armstrong wanted to be there with his friends. Dozens of girls wanted to go with him. He could have had his pick, but he had to pay for his mistake. You see, one thing his parents would not allow was talking back to teachers. When Woodcock told Nick's parents what he said, they punished him hard. Not only was he prohibited from going to the dance, but he was grounded for two weeks on top of that.

We always marveled at Nick's inexhaustible energy. When we were kids, he never sat still. He played baseball with his cousins in the morning, basketball with us in the afternoon, and then football with his neighbors in the evening. He never stopped. All those hours of endless physical activity had garnered him a body chiseled like a statue. He had a very powerful physique. I used to joke with him by saying my mom wanted to know if I could bring over a load of laundry to clean on his washboard stomach. He loved that one.

The basement of his house, which he had converted into his own private gym, was equipped with an entire weight set. The walls surrounding him were adorned with posters of his favorite football teams. However, the ceiling was the most interesting part. Directly above his workout bench hung a shrine of nearly a hundred pictures and newspaper clippings of his favorite athlete— running back, Jim Brown. He kept them hidden there so only he could see them when he was doing his bench-press routine.

Brown was a first-class athlete just like Nick. He was well-built, could play every sport, and play each one well. Because he was a black athlete, Brown had to work twice as hard to get half the credit. The fact that Nick recognized the awesome hardships and successes of the Syracuse University graduate showed he viewed football as much more than just a game.

As he sat on the edge of the bench in his dimly-lit basement, he could not help but reflect on all he was missing out on. It hurt him. It hurt him badly. He stood up and added more weight—time to get back to work.

"C'mon, push yourself! Push yourself!" Woodcock...his parents...the football coach...the girls at the dance...it all ripped through his head like a tornado, obliterating the corners of his mind. "Nine...ten..." He counted the repetitions out loud to try to keep his mind focused on the weights, but it did not help much. "Fifteen...sixteen..." There in his basement, Nick exorcised his demons and shared an evening of segregation with his idol— denied, neglected, and misunderstood. "Twenty-four...twenty-five..." As Nick finished the last set, he reached over onto a small desk and while pushing his football playbook aside, picked up his Bible. He stared at it for a moment and then set it back down.

Then he flipped the switch on his radio and introduced Jim to Rock 'N' Roll.

"Bah, bah, bah, bah
bah, bah, bah, bah
bah, bah, bah, bah,
bah, bah, bah, bah, at the hop!
Well, you can rock it, you can roll it,
Do the stomp, and even stroll it, at the hop, bop, bop, bop."

We must have danced for an hour straight before we decided to take a break. The sock hop was a huge success. Lana Lorenza, the head of the Homecoming Committee, looked thrilled. She heard endless compliments about the decorations, which she and her committee members worked on tirelessly all week. The music was hip, the dancing was hot, and the refreshments were cold.

Elizabeth and Deke made it a point to dance in front, behind, between, next to, and practically on top of Kimmie and me. Of course, they were always dancing "inappropriately" as my mother would say. It was just another way of God explaining life to me. They were his puppets. Sadly enough a puppet master can never perform well when the puppets want to control the strings themselves. My hunch told me sooner or later they would be cut loose.

Oddly enough, I happened to see Deke Marshall walk over to the punch bowl and pour a bottle into it that he had pulled from the inside pocket of his jacket. I struggled with the idea of telling one of the chaperones, but I did not have to because the Vice Principal saw the whole thing and personally escorted him and Elizabeth down to his office. I suppose he called their parents from there. They were forced to call it a night early. Charles's instincts were proven correct once again.

The band announced they had worked out a brand new song by Buddy Holly. It was a beautiful, new ballad. Lana Lorenza got on the microphone and announced it was time to do "The Stroll." Everyone formed two lines. It was a cool way for everybody to get together and show off their date to the crowd. This was a moment I had dreaded all week. I had even planned to come up with a way of getting lost just at the right time so I would not have to go through with it. But when the time came, Kimmie and I were the first two in line.

The way it works is each couple starts at one end and walks through the long tunnel of people. They "stroll" down the aisle. They face each other and then go back to back and repeat this over and over again. Everyone lines up on either side and sways back and forth until it is their turn to walk through the "tunnel of love." It is always good fun because it gets everyone involved.

As I walked through with Kimmie, I saw a lot of people smiling at us. They were starting to realize we were a class act after all and we should be treated accordingly. She looked so delighted to be part of the action. I had never seen her so happy. The ladies' hearts melted when the saxophone player did his solo. I knew that song would be a classic.

THIRTEEN

"The best and most beautiful things in the world cannot be seen or even touched – they must be felt with the heart."

HELEN KELLER

Seven blocks away from school, a young man lay on his bed staring off into space. Porter did not go to dances. He did not go to football games or talent shows. Porter was not able to do very much on the weekends and many of us knew enough not to ask why. He bounced a tennis ball off the wall in front of him over and over again. The hypnotic rhythm dulled his senses. A cigarette burned in an ashtray he kept on his windowsill. He took extreme measures to hide the habit from his father.

I had only been in Porter's room once when his dad was at work. I was amazed by a bookcase full of classics he had read. I saw beautiful, leather-bound editions of *The Complete Works of William Shakespeare*, Edgar Allan Poe's *Collection of Short Stories*, and Arthur Conan Doyle's *Sherlock Holmes Mysteries*. He had read them all cover to cover. I was shocked Porter was into fiction and drama until he explained to me that they were his mother's and reading them made him feel closer to her. Of course, there were a couple of books about sports and hunting too. There was no doubt Porter was an intellectual. He just never wanted to be labeled as anything by anyone.

There were piles of dirty dishes under his bed and a huge mound of clothes in the corner. Carelessly strewn about the place were Moon Pie wrappers—one of his favorite snacks—and Coca-Cola bottles. Amid all the chaos was his shotgun for hunting which delicately balanced on two wooden pegs near his bed. It was remarkably shiny and impressive. This was the only pristine area of the room. Above it hung a few hunting awards he procured in contests over the years.

After counting three hundred tosses of the ball, he rolled over and reached under his mattress. He pulled out a magazine filled with pictures of beautiful, naked women. He listlessly leafed through it without much satisfaction. Then he suddenly came across a picture he had stuffed in there. It was the farewell shot of

Humphrey Bogart and Ingrid Bergman from the film *Casablanca*. This particular picture struck him and he lost himself in reverie once again. He started to quietly whistle the theme song from the film. *"You must remember this, a kiss is still a kiss..."*

There was something about the timeless couple that mesmerized Porter. He knew, if given a chance, he could wield that same magic that Bogart so effortlessly possessed. Someday he would have his chance to play the hero to a beautiful damsel in distress. Someday he would capture her in his arms and tell her she would be better off without him. Except when he played the part, the woman would not be able to leave him. He wondered if he would ever find a woman like that. Slowly his mind drifted seven blocks away to the school gymnasium. He leaned over and reached onto his nightstand and turned on his radio, pretending he was there.

"Take out the papers and the trash,
or you don't get no spendin' cash,
if you don't scrub that kitchen floor,
you ain't gonna Rock 'N' Roll no more,
Yakety Yak, Don't Talk Back!"

As he listened to the music he wondered what his friends were doing. Then he heard the front door slam. It shook the house and knocked the radio off the edge of the nightstand and onto the floor. Frank Sr. was home. With every stair he ascended, Porter prayed that night would be a good one. Maybe his father had been working late or maybe he only had a couple of drinks.

The door flew open. "What are you doin' in here, Frank?" A giant of a man stood in the center of the doorway.

"Nothin', sir. Just listenin' to some music," Porter said as he gently put the radio back onto the windowsill, hiding his cigarette from view. Those anxious moments were when he missed his mother the most. His father was so unpredictable. The key was not to make direct eye contact.

"What're ya listenin' to? 'Take out the papers and the trash?' What a stupid song. Well...Did you take out the trash today?" His speech was slurred.

"No, sir. It's not garbage day. I take it out every Tuesday, remember?" Porter said. He caught a glimpse of his father out of the corner of his eye. He wore a three-day-old beard, a torn, sleeveless undershirt splattered with grease stains, and a pair of camouflaged hunting pants.

"Are you gettin' smart with me?" he said with a strange smile on his face. Then he started toward his son.

"No, sir. Not at all." He stared at his father's bronco belt buckle, shining from the reflection of the small lamp next to his bed. He had seen it in his dreams.

"This place is a mess. Clean it up!" He stumbled around the room. Porter knew his father's room was ten times as bad, but with Frank Porter Sr. it was always "Do as I say, not as I do." Young Porter looked around and realized it was worse than usual. He had forgotten to care.

"D'ya think I work to put food on the table and a roof over your head so you can disrespect me like this? You lazy, good-for-nothin' kid. You don't appreciate me...you're just like your mother. She never gave a damn about me either." Porter's mom went out for groceries one day and never returned. She bore a hole in her son's heart that could never be filled. He was only seven years old.

"I'll get the room clean. Now, why don't you go downstairs and get somethin' to eat." The smell of alcohol emanating from his father nearly gagged him.

"You tryin' to get rid of me? You don't even wanna talk to your own father, do you, you little delinquent?"

"No, sir. That's not true, but I just know you haven't eaten yet, that's all," Porter said, backing up into the corner of his room.

"I got a call from your principal today. D'ya know what he had to say?" They stood toe-to-toe.

Porter knew no answer was the right answer. When Frank Sr. was in the wrong mood, he did not need an excuse to take it out on his son. When Frank Sr. got fired, Porter's grades suddenly were not good enough. When Frank Sr. totaled his car, Porter had not mopped the kitchen floor to his liking. Old Man Crutcher called about the incident with Bulbsey, and Porter knew it meant imminent pain.

Frank Sr. was quite the boxer in his day. He had a keen sense for smelling fear in his opponent. He had his son on the ropes and it would not be just another sparring session. The lights came up and Frank Sr. stood center ring. He would show this rookie a thing or two about messing with the heavyweight champ. As he closed in on Porter, Frank Sr. stopped momentarily and turned the volume up on the radio so the neighbors could not hear. The bell rang for round one.

"You made...me cry...when you said...good bye
Ain't that a shame...my tears fell like rain.
Ain't that a shame...you're the one to blame."

The band finally got around to playing some Fats Domino. The lead singer of the band stepped up to the microphone and announced, "This one's goin' out to Elizabeth from her good friend, Chris."

Charles smiled at me and shouted over the noise, "I couldn't resist." There was a chorus of laughter. People were patting me on the back and nodding in approval at Kimmie. She looked ecstatic. We were all having a great time. A few girls even stopped to compliment Kimmie on her outfit. They were going out of their way to take sides against the "too cool" crowd. Just when I thought things could not get any better, they ripped into an Elvis song.

"The warden through a party in the county jail.
The prison band was there and they began to wail.
The band was jumpin' and the joint began to swing.
You should've heard those knocked out jailbirds sing, let's rock."

Jack and Drew came running out onto the dance floor with their dates. "No one's gonna dance to an Elvis song without me!" Jack shouted. As soon as the crowd saw him coming, they cleared the way. Drew joined in a big circle that spontaneously formed around his buddy. Jack was wearing this incredible charcoal gray suit with a pink shirt and black tie. It was just like the one Elvis wore on the Ed Sullivan Show. Jack was amazing. He slid across the floor on his knees and then jumped up onto his feet. Everyone joined in, cheering him on.

He did a split and came up out of it with ease. His body moved like a toy doll. Every move was effortless. He did spins and twists and turns that made the crowd roar. It was as if he were a celebrity. People watched in amazement. It was Jack's moment to shine.

He danced across the floor, moving his hips and feet just like Elvis. He ended up over by his date, Theresa. She patiently waited for him. He grabbed her and they went into this routine in perfect synchronization. It was really something to see. I looked across the circle and saw Mary and her friends shouting and cheering alongside Charles and Anna. Everyone loved when Jack performed.

He took Theresa and threw her up in the air and swung her around his back and then they flew across the floor together. He twirled her left and then right and at one point he launched her up in the air and she did a perfect backflip. The crowd went wild. She danced across to the center of the circle.

For the grand finale, Jack ran up to her and jumped over her five-foot frame with his legs spread. He landed in a perfect split, came up out of it, turned, and grabbed her in time to dip her on the last beat of the song. They received an enormous round of applause. I had never seen anything like it.

Everyone rushed into the center of the circle. Kimmie and I joined Charles and Anna. We waited for Jack's fans to part.

"That was incredible, Jack!"

"Thanks, Charles."

"I'm so proud of my little brother. I wish Mom and Dad were here," Anna said as she leaned over and wiped the sweat from his brow.

"Jack, you were amazing as always. You know my date, Kimmie, don't you?"

"Sure. I know Kimmie. How are ya? Why would a girl like you wanna come to the dance with this guy?"

"He's been a perfect gentleman all night. You're an outstanding dancer. You have so much life in your body. I can't think of anything I can do that well."

"Thank you, honey. That's nice of you to say. Oh, hey, everybody, how 'bout my date, Theresa? Isn't she great?" He was so different from the guy we played around with on the Funball field. He was a true Gemini—split personality.

Drew introduced everyone to his date, Kathy. We tried our best to muster up a polite hello. We all knew she was leading him on. She would do things like ask him to a dance on Friday and then she would be dating some other guy on Monday. We did not like her very much, but we tried not to interfere, knowing how Drew felt about her.

"Well, guess what happened to the good old Edsel?" Drew asked. "It broke down. That's why we're so late. Jack kicked the fender so hard the license plate fell off. The only way I could get him to calm down was I put the car in neutral and let him see how far he could push it. He got it about five houses down the street until he finally quit. We tried and tried to get it started and then we just decided to walk. My feet are still killin' me."

"Well, I guess we'll have to just dance to the romantic, slow songs then," Kathy said. No one was amused.

Kimmie broke the uncomfortable silence, "Chris, I need to use the ladies' room. I'll be right back."

"Oh, I need to go too. I'll come along with you, Kimmie," Anna said.

"I need to get somethin' to drink."

"Try the punch, Jack. I hear it's great," Charles said. I smiled and explained the joke. The band slowed things down again with a ballad. Those on the floor without partners started to disperse when I heard a few girls behind me giggling.

"Hey, Chris. I think those girls wanna ask you to dance. See 'em...the blond and the brunette," Charles said.

"Really? Nah. They're talkin' about Jack, don't ya think?"

"The one on the right pointed at you and the one on the left smiled. Besides, they've been starin' at you for about five minutes straight now."

"They're probably talkin' about me and Kimmie."

"I don't know, Chris. I think bringin' Kimmie to this dance was a real good idea. I've heard quite a few people say nice things about the two of you. Wait...here they come. I'll get lost."

"Hi, Chris. My friend and I just wanted you to know we think you're a great dancer," the blond said with an embarrassed smile.

"Thanks. That's nice of you to say. I'm nothin' like my cousin, though."

"We both wanna dance with you, but we can't decide who should ask you first. Could you end this argument and just pick one of us?" the brunette asked.

"I'm very flattered ladies, but you want me to pick..." I blushed and suddenly I felt someone come up from behind and take my hand.

"Sorry, ladies, but you'll have to try back later. This dance belongs to me."

As I turned around I wound up face to face with Julia, Yorkie's waitress. I had seen Julia a million times before, but never like that. I barely recognized her without her nametag on her shirt.

"Hey, Julia! How ya doin'?"

"I'm fine."

"You're fine all right. That's some dress you've got on there." She wore this gorgeous black dress. Her hair was very long and wavy. I never knew she hid all of that up under her waitress cap. She wore this incredible, red lipstick that matched her fingernails and a gold necklace accompanied by a pair of gold earrings. She looked like a model. I could not believe it. I took her by the hand and we began to sway to the music.

"What? D'ya think I look funny not wearin' my waitress uniform?"

"No. I wasn't thinkin' of you wearin' anything."

"Huh?"

"I mean...uh...not that I was thinking of you wearing nothing...I mean...what I was trying to say is...you look beautiful."

She sensed my embarrassment and smiled. "You havin' fun tonight?"

"Definitely. Who'd you come here with?"

"You know Don, don't you? He works the grill at Yorkie's."

"Oh, Don...yeah, I know him. I came with Kimmie."

"I know. She's a very nice girl, a lot nicer than that Elizabeth Allen."

"How'd ya know about me and Elizabeth?"

"Are you kiddin'? Everyone at school has been talkin' about it all week."

"How come I haven't seen you around school?"

100

"Well, I don't have any classes with you and I guess our paths never really cross. But you walk right by my locker every day when you go to English class."

"Really? I guess I wouldn't miss you if you had a burger and milkshake in your hands."

"Ha…Ha…very funny. You know, I've been watchin' you here tonight and I noticed somethin' about you. You're very close to your family, aren't you?"

"Yeah. Why do you ask?" I spun her around gently and then brought her back in close.

"Because I just realized you came with your brother and your cousin who you've been hanging out with all night. And you were just cheering your cousin on out on the dance floor."

"Yeah. I love all those guys. My family is very important to me. You only have one, ya know? Do you have any siblings?"

"I have an older sister. We're very close just like you guys are. Family is very important to me too. My parents are constantly telling me, 'Julia, always make room in your life for God, family, and school.'"

"Wow! This is scary. Did you ask my brother about all the things I want in a woman or somethin'?"

She laughed. "No. Why? Do you agree with me?"

"Right on the money. I still can't believe I've never seen you at school." I spun her around again and brought her body back in close. She smelled great. Her little hands felt soft and warm. "I can't believe you're here. I thought you worked at Yorkie's every night."

"He was kind enough to give us tonight off. I'm actually gonna stop in later to pick up my paycheck."

"So this guy, Don…are you two…goin' together?"

She paused to keep me in suspense. "No…we're just good friends. Are you and Kimmie goin' together?"

"No…we're just good friends too. We've gone to school together ever since I can remember. Hey, how come I don't remember you going to grade school with us back in the day?"

"My family moved here from Rochester two years ago. You and I didn't go to the same Junior High because I live over on Roosevelt Avenue, but when I made it to ninth grade I went to

Wilson just like everybody else. It's kind of a long walk home to be honest."

"You walk home?"

"Yeah, most of the time. Why?"

"Maybe I could walk you home sometime? I don't mind a long walk. What d'ya say?"

"Sure. Just let me know. Stop by my locker sometime at the end of the day. By the way, I don't need to have a tray of food in my hands for you to recognize me, do I?"

"No...I think I'll be able to spot you in a crowd from now on," I said. We danced quietly for the next few minutes. I reflected on all the surprises the night had brought me. Julia and I stood very close to one another. Her body was comforting. I had been around her every week for the past two years, but I never truly saw her until that night.

~ FOURTEEN ~

"We are confronted primarily with a moral issue. It is as old as the Scriptures and is as clear as the American Constitution."
JOHN F. KENNEDY

We decided to stay until the very last song because everyone was having such a good time. We left to meet up with the rest of the gang right after the band packed up around ten o'clock. We had just enough time to get over to Yorkie's for an ice cream sundae. Jack and Drew had to split so they could figure out what to do with my aunt's Edsel.

On the way home we saw Porter and Nick standing on a street corner. I told Charles to drop me off a few houses down. He turned off his lights, pulled over, and killed the engine. They did not seem to notice we were even there. I slowly crept up on them from the darkness underneath the trees.

I tried my best impersonation of a police officer. "You boys got any I.D.?"

"Huh? Aw...Chris! You scared the crap outta me! What the hell are ya doin' here? Aren't you supposed to be at the dance?" Nick said. Porter never flinched.

"Nah. It's over. It's a little after ten. Hey, Porter, did I spook ya even a little?" I asked.

"Not one bit, but it was a good try."

"Hey, the dance wasn't the same without you guys. Charles and I were just gonna come find you to see if you wanna join us at Yorkie's for ice cream. What d'ya think?"

"Can't ya see we're busy?" Porter said.

"What d'ya mean? What's goin' on?"

"Look at that," Nick said and pointed across the street. Behind the house across the street and just to the right, I could see the back of an apartment building. I noticed a light on in one of the upstairs bedrooms.

"Yeah...I see a light on in the upstairs room of that apartment. So what?"

"Keep watchin', Slick," Porter said, barely moving his lips. I stared at the window with them for a moment and suddenly a figure moved into our field of vision and stopped, giving us a clear view of a woman. It was not just any woman. It was Ms. Turner, the famous beauty who worked at the bank. All of us guys brought her dozens of rolls of coins to change into bills just to smell her perfume. She was giving a free, private show every guy in town would pay good money for.

"Oh...my...God! Is that who I think it is?" I asked.

"You better believe it," Porter said.

"You should've been here ten minutes ago when I first bumped into Porter. She was just gettin' started. First she took off her shoes, then the jewelry, then the blouse."

"You know what's comin' off next?" Porter asked.

"I can't believe it. This is wrong though guys. We shouldn't be here. We're...we're...invading...her... privacy," I said as I squinted to see better.

"Don't worry, she's not gonna find out. In a few minutes she's gonna turn off the light and then go to bed," Porter said.

"How d'ya know all that?" Nick asked.

"Just trust me...I know. Now shut up. Here comes the best part."

"Look at that body. I can't believe God could make somethin' that perfect," Nick said.

"Holy mackerel! She's gonna take off her bra. I just know it," I said. We all focused intensely like FBI agents trying to spot a sniper on a rooftop.

"Oh, God, please don't strike me blind now," Nick said.

"What's she gotta do, unbutton it?" I asked.

"No, you fool. It's probably got a hook. Quiet! Here she goes...here she goes," Porter said as all three of us leaned in. She reached around her back and started to unfasten it.

"Hey, what are you guys starin' at?" Charles's voice shocked us all into spasm. When we turned around Charles was standing there with Anna and Kimmie closing in on us.

Anna called out, "What are you goofballs up to now?" Charles caught a quick glimpse of "Venus" in the window and abruptly turned to the ladies. Nick and I blocked the girls' view. Porter never moved an inch.

"Nothing to see here, believe me! We were all just gonna cram into the car and head over to Yorkie's, right guys?" Charles said.

"Yeah. That's right. In fact, we should all get goin', right Porter?" I said.

"Uh huh. I suppose so." The lights went off. The show was over. "Okay, let's go. I'm starvin'. Anybody else in the mood for one of Yorkie's sundaes?"

"We just gotta stop and pick up Goodie on the way. Kimmie, I'll make sure my baby brother has you home by eleven. Is that okay?" Charles asked.

"That's fine. I'm havin' a great time. Besides, I've never had one of Yorkie's sundaes. Are they good?"

"Never had one of Yorkie's sundaes? Well, I guess you've waited long enough," I said as I opened the car door for her. All six of us piled in.

We picked up Goodie on the way and officially set a new record for my uncle's car, three in front and four in back. One time Porter took his old man's Mercury when he was out cold and we crammed fourteen of us into it. It sounded like a good idea at the time.

The evening was coming to a close and I could not complain about the way it turned out. I even had a few bucks to cover the ice cream for Kimmie and me. Her old man sure was a nice guy. As we entered Yorkie's, I noticed that he looked very distracted and nervous. He was talking to these two black kids who went to our school named Michael and Sam.

They both were well-dressed and had pretty girls holding onto them. They must have come straight from the dance. I never got to know them very well, but I heard they were nice guys. They were two of our school's track stars. There was one story floating around school about Michael getting into a fight with this big jerk who threw the shot put. Other than that, we did not know anything else about them.

Yorkie threw us a quick glance and then went back to his conversation with Michael and Sam, "You boys don't understand. I got some important people in here. The judge's family is at table four eatin' ice cream and my meat supplier's family is slurpin' down milkshakes at table five. They would not like it very much if a couple guys like you sat down next to them at this hour of the night. Believe me, it's nothin' personal, but I got a business to run."

"It is personal, Yorkie! Who d'ya think you're kiddin'?" Michael said. The two girls stared down at the floor.

"You know that's not true. I let you guys in here all the time, but tonight's a bad night. Why don't ya go to the diner a few blocks down, huh?"

"Because we're here now and it's gettin' late. If we're good enough to eat here during the day, why aren't we good enough to eat here at night?" Sam asked.

"When you boys get older you'll understand. I'm sorry, but that's the way it is."

We all heard the conversation as we entered the restaurant. We kind of quietly slithered past them. No one said a word. I knew my dad would tell me to stay out of it, but deep down I also knew that was just because he wanted to protect us. My parents understood these little incidents were obviously wrong. However, they also knew it could mean a ton of trouble for us if we got involved. My mother always taught me to follow my heart and my father always taught me there was a time and a place for everything.

I looked at Charles, "We gotta do somethin'," I said.

He stopped walking and let out an audible sigh. I could see he was struggling with the decision. Then a smile suddenly came over his face as he turned toward Michael and Sam.

"Hey, there you guys are. We've been lookin' all over for you," he said as he started toward them. They looked surprised and did not know what to think. They still had their defenses up.

I walked over and shook their hands, "Michael, Sam, ladies. It's good to see ya. We lost you after we left the dance. We should've followed you over, but we're all here now. Yorkie, we're gonna need the big booth in the corner by the jukebox and that long table next to it. We got, oh let's see, how many people, one-two-three..." I talked so fast Yorkie did not have a second to interrupt.

"C'mon let's go and join the others," Charles said as he guided all four of them past Yorkie and over to the table with the rest of the gang. One of the best things about our friends was we always stood up for one another. Charles and I knew the rest of the gang would support our decision.

"Nine-ten-eleven. We've got a party of eleven, okay, Yorkie? We're awful hungry so you better get that grill fired up. And some of us even have a little extra cash for ice cream too so don't lock up the freezer just yet," I said with a smile.

He stared at me with a defeated look and said, "You got it. Now go join your friends. I'll have someone out to take your order in a minute. I'm a bit understaffed because I gave Julia the night off."

"Julia." She jumped back into my mind. "Oh, yeah, I saw her earlier tonight. She looked great. We shared a dance."

"Yeah? What are the odds of that?" he said with a wink. "She'll be in a bit later to pick up her paycheck. I'll send her over." I loved that old man.

"Thanks, York. I'm sure we could add one more to our party. Let me know when she gets here, okay? Thanks again...for everything," I said.

"No problem. By the way, lucky for you, I'm in a good mood because the Yankees won tonight. Mantle hit a walk-off homer in the ninth. You can tell your friend, Porter, that Mickey, Mickey, got a big stickey," he said as he went back into the kitchen. "Let's move boys, we got hungry people out here," he shouted to his employees.

I walked right past the judge's table and noticed him staring. He looked up at me so I gave him a big smile and said, "Good evening, your honor."

He smiled back at me and said, "Hello, young man." He went back to eating his ice cream. By the time I got over to the booth, the gang was engrossed in conversation.

"So you hit em'? Right in the face? I don't believe it. Why?" Nick asked Michael as Goodie and Porter listened in.

"Well. He made some unpleasant remarks, if you know what I mean, about Jim Brown. You don't do that in front of me. He's my man," Michael said.

"You're kiddin'? Jim Brown is my all-time favorite athlete. I'm tellin' these guys all the time how he's the best ever. Ya know, he's gonna win the MVP this year. It's in the bag," Nick said.

"Hey, if you like Jim Brown you'll love the new running back Syracuse just picked up out of Elmira. His name is Ernie Davis. I hear he's even gonna wear #44 just like Brown. He's gonna be somethin', all right," Michael said.

Meanwhile, Sam was telling Charles about the school record he just set in hurdles. Both of these guys were exceptional athletes. More importantly, they were very nice guys. Their dates seemed real nice too.

Anna leaned over toward Michael's girl and asked, "Did you have a good time tonight?"

"You better believe it. I don't have many opportunities to dress up like this. Michael didn't really wanna go, but when I told him he didn't have a choice in the matter he changed his tune. I said, 'Michael, we've been datin' for a year now and you haven't taken me out dancin' once. Go buy yourself some nice clothes 'cause we're goin' to that dance!' That was all there was to it. By the way, I'm Diana and this is Martha," she said.

"It's nice to meet you both. I'm Anna and this is Kimmie."

"I know you, Kimmie. You're the smartest one in my science class," Martha said.

"I do okay," Kimmie said. "I love your dress. It's beautiful. If it's not too personal...could you tell me how you put on your make-up? It looks so professional." We went on talking for about twenty minutes. It's amazing how much you can find in common with people when you just take the time to get to know them.

FIFTEEN

"All the resources we need are in the mind."
                                    THEODORE ROOSEVELT

It suddenly dawned on us that we had developed quite an appetite after dancing all evening. We decided we needed something more than just dessert so we ordered burgers and fries. All of us guys inhaled them without a word. We listened to the ladies talk as we raced through our meals. I was looking at the dessert menu before Kimmie even took a bite.

Charles wanted to bide some time for the ladies so he asked me to tell everyone a story.

"Oh, that's a great idea. Chris tells the best stories. You gotta hear one of 'em," Anna said.

"What kinda stories?" Michael asked.

"I like when Chris tells funny stories about the teachers at school," Goodie said.

"Nah...the best ones are all those from the neighborhood when we were kids," Nick added.

"I think I know a good one Chris could tell," Charles said with a mischievous grin. "Why don't you tell 'The Legend of Shoonuckha?'"

"Oh, no! That one gave me nightmares," Goodie said.

"Oh, great! It's a scary one. Chris tells the best scary stories," Anna said.

"I don't know. Are you sure I should tell that one?" I teased. I wanted to tell it, but something was missing.

"Hey gang!" We heard a voice from over by the jukebox. It was Julia. Everyone was just as surprised as I was when they saw how beautiful she looked all dressed up. Charles made room for her at the end of the table so she and I sat directly across from each other. Everything was all set.

"So are you gonna tell the story or not?" Porter asked. Anna clued Julia in as to what was going on and then they all sat there quietly. I felt like a kindergarten teacher, facing a room full of kids sitting on their mats.

"I should warn them first, Chris. As scary and unbelievable as this story may seem, everything you'll hear is absolutely true," Charles said. Diana and Martha moved in closer to their dates. The restaurant had pretty much emptied out. We had about fifteen minutes until close—just enough time for me to create some magic.

"When my father was a kid he heard this story called 'The Legend of Shoonuckha.' Shoonuckha was an Indian Chief of the Onondaga tribe. The Onondagas populated this entire area of central New York. Many years ago when the settlers first came to this country, they took thousands of acres of land that belonged to the Indians. They pushed them around, hoping they'd all die off or run away, leaving the land behind. There were many bloody battles and many lives lost.

"Shoonuckha had a wife and two children, a boy and a girl. They tried their best to stay away from the settlers. One day when Shoonuckha's two children were out pickin' berries they ran into a few of the white men. The children ran, screaming for their father as the men pursued them.

"Legend has it that when Shoonuckha saw his children bein' chased, he sent his spirit into a hawk. It dropped down out of the sky and plucked the men's eyes out. They lived the rest of their lives in darkness. When the children and their mother returned home, they couldn't find Shoonuckha anywhere. He returned days later, without any explanation." I could see everyone was paying close attention to the details.

"Another time Shoonuckha and his wife and kids were down by the river. His wife was cleanin' the family's clothes while the children played and he did some fishin'. He wandered downstream a bit to find the best spot. After a while, he decided to go check on his family. As he returned, he saw a group of men surrounding his wife.

"Legend has it that he sent his spirit out—this time into a bear. It suddenly appeared with a thunderous growl. The children reported that it tore the men limb from limb. Their body parts were strewn all over the ground. The woman was left completely untouched. It was days before Shoonuckha returned home and once again there was no explanation." Goodie sat wincing over in the corner.

110

"Unfortunately, the friends of all the men who were injured or killed were convinced Shoonuckha was responsible for all this. They snuck up on him in the middle of the night, knocked him unconscious, and tied him to a stake. When he awoke, he discovered his entire family had been slaughtered. He looked the killers in the eyes and said, 'You have taken from me everything that matters in my life. After I am dead and gone I will find a way to get to each and every one of you and make you suffer the way you have made me suffer.' They laughed. With the strike of a match, the flame ignited and engulfed his body."

"That's awful," Anna said.

"That's incredible...So what happened? Did he come back and kill everybody?" Michael asked.

"Well, legend further states that over the next year everyone responsible for the killings of Shoonuckha's family wound up dead. One guy was devoured by a wolf...another bitten by a snake...a third trampled by a buffalo. One by one they all died under mysterious circumstances."

"Tell 'em about the reservoir, Chris," Nick said.

"Yeah, here's where I should explain the reservoir. The reservoir is a huge hill, filled with water, that's fenced off at the top to keep away trespassers. Some people think Shoonuckha's ghost is up there, far away from everyone and he dwells there to this day. People used to swear they saw his shadow in the moonlight. Some even say on a calm night...if you listen closely enough...you can hear his Indian drum beating."

"You mean the reservoir a few blocks past school?" Sam asked.

"That's the one," answered Charles.

"Here's where it really starts to get good, sports fans."

"This is the part where my father comes into the story. When he was in high school he went up to the rez with his friends on a dare. In his day, the story that circulated was that if the legend were told while sitting on the top of the rez, then old Shoonuckha would suddenly appear." I noticed one by one, Yorkie and his employees found a way to take a seat nearby after they finished clearing off the tables.

"It was a hot August night and my dad and his pals decided to tackle the hill. They wanted to see if old Shoonuckha was really up there. My father sat encircled by his friends and went into great detail about 'The Legend of Shoonuckha.' After they all heard the story they ventured up farther toward the top of the hill. When they got there, they saw this small, brick building on the other side of the fence. Charles, do you remember what it was for?"

"Yeah. Dad said it was where all the electricity kept the filtering system workin' or somethin' like that. It looked like a brick shed. It wasn't even that big."

I continued, "Right. It wasn't all that big. The top of the fence had barbed wire all around it so they decided to be daredevils and crawl under the fence, which was covered with 'Do Not Enter' signs. The fence had a weak spot. They succeeded and headed over to the brick building.

"My father said that when they entered the building they saw a very small room with a stairway in the middle of it that went straight down. He and his friends agreed whoever went down the stairway would get a Marble Farms' chocolate milkshake paid for by the others. Well, my father was addicted to those milkshakes. He couldn't resist." The girls were drawing in closer and closer to everyone else. Julia smiled at me from across the table.

"When he got to the bottom of the stairs he flipped a switch and the lights went on. The hallways had little lights hanging from the ceiling in a perfectly straight line. He realized he was underneath the rez, looking at a series of connected tunnels like in a maze. My father was fascinated. He said there was something exciting about being in a place so close to home no one else had ever seen.

"He walked down to the end of one hallway and when it ended, he took a left. Then he went to the end of another hallway and took a right. Then he noticed it started getting really hot. He was closing in on what he thought was some kind of a boiler room. There were all kinds of pipes, and levers, and big tanks that looked like furnaces. And that's when it happened."

"Oh, God. What happened? Did it flood or somethin'?" Diana asked.

"The lights flickered on and off and then he heard the sound of a drum...an Indian drum." I drummed on the table with my hands. DAH...dah...dah...dah. I paused for effect and then I continued drumming on the table again, with increasing speed.

DAH…dah…dah…dah… DAH…dah…dah…dah. "He froze in horror. 'Shoonuckha…it must be Shoonuckha,' he thought. He turned and started to run. The drumming continued," I said as the boys started pounding. DAH…dah…dah…dah…DAH…dah…dah…dah.

I raised the volume and pitch of my voice. "He ran down the end of the hallway, but he couldn't remember where to go next. Did he make a right? Then goin' back should he make a left? If he made a left, then going back should he make a right?" The drumming on the table got even louder. DAH…dah…dah…dah… DAH…dah…dah…dah.

"He scrambled for his life and finally he could hear his friends yelling for him. He went toward their voices until he saw the staircase he originally descended. The drumming got louder and faster." DAH…dah…dah…dah…DAH…dah…dah…dah… "As he made it to the top, his friends saw the terror on his face and were immediately petrified. He blew past them and out the door. The gang quickly followed him in a panic. They scrambled under the fence, stumbled down the hill, and ran all the way home."

"Did he see anything?" Anna asked.

"He said he never saw anything, but he's convinced to this day he heard that drum and it must've been Shoonuckha's ghost. None of his friends ever went back to find out," I said.

"That's a great story!" Michael said.

"Yeah, that was terrific. Wasn't it, hun?" Sam said, looking at Martha.

"I'm scared now. You better walk me to the door tonight when you drop me off," she said and slapped his arm.

"You too, Mister. I'm not ever goin' anywhere alone at night again, and I mean ever," Diana said and we all laughed.

"That's definitely a classic," Nick said.

"I get goose bumps every single time I hear it," Goodie said.

"You haven't even heard the best part yet," interrupted Porter.

"Yeah, Chris. Tell 'em what the four of us did," Charles said.

"There's more? I don't know if I wanna hear it if it gets any worse."

"Don't worry, Kimmie. Chris and I will both make sure you get home safe and sound. Go ahead, Chris."

"There was this spectacular meteor shower the weatherman on the news had been talkin' about for days. It was supposed to be this incredible display of shooting stars. We didn't want to miss it, so we figured the rez was a perfect place to witness such a thing. It's a place of high elevation and on a clear night you can see for miles, straight across the city of Syracuse. So two of my foolish friends here, Nick and Goodie, joined Charles and me as we headed out to see what the buzz was all about." I took a sip of water.

Charles took over, "The only problem was that it was gonna take place around midnight. My baby brother and his friends were only in junior high. We didn't even bother askin' Mom and Dad 'cause we knew they'd never let us go. So we all agreed to sneak out of the house and meet at the rez just before midnight."

"How come you weren't there, Porter?" Anna asked.

"I was helpin' my dad with somethin' and I couldn't get away," he said as he sheepishly covered a fresh bruise on his left cheek.

I spoke over the awkward silence. "So we all met around midnight. I remember it was a Thursday, the twelfth of August. Anyway, we all went up to the very top of the hill to find the best spot. There was a 'Do Not Enter' sign hangin' right behind us on the barbed-wire fence.

"After about ten minutes of starin' at the sky and not seein' a single shooting star, I turned to Nick and Goodie and asked, 'Did you guys ever hear about, "The Legend of Shoonuckha?"' Charles immediately jumped in and begged me not to tell it. But his apprehension made Nick and Goodie wanna hear it all the more. So they sat there and I told them the entire story. After I finished, Nick said, 'I wonder if that weak spot on the fence is still there.' Before long we were all talkin' about goin' up under the fence. My wise brother here was the only one smart enough not to venture under it."

"Your mother would be proud, Charles," Anna said.

"Well, I figured somebody had to play it safe."

"Right. Well, Nick and I practically dragged Goodie up the hill and then we found the weak spot. We were under the fence in a matter of seconds and standin' on the illegal side like my father had done thirty years before. We slowly walked up and soon we saw the roof of the brick building. No one said a word. Our hearts started pumpin' as we made it to the top. At the precise moment we reached the water, a hundred birds flew up into our faces. You wanna talk about scared?" I laughed.

"Goodie nearly crapped his pants if I remember hearin' correctly," Porter said.

"No I didn't. I'll admit I was scared, but these guys were too. We all screamed," he said for the record.

Then Goodie continued with the story, "We yelled down to Charles so he'd know what happened and then we stared out at this immense body of water. The top of the rez was like a private lake hidden away from everyone. The flat surface of the water drew a perfect line across the horizon. It was impressive. The water looked pitch-black. The thought of someone fallin' in sent a shiver down my spine. We all made sure we didn't get too close to the edge.

"Across the water you could see the lights of the city reflecting up into the sky. We decided to take a lap around the top so we could get a closer look. Then on our way back around we spent a few minutes yellin' out 'echo' down into the valley and waitin' to hear our own reply. Nick, you wanna tell 'em what happened next?"

"Sure. I remember Charles begged us once again to come down from the top before someone got hurt. Chris and I both wanted to get into that building before the night was over, but we decided to go back under the fence to prevent Charles from worrying. As we crawled back under the fence, my shirt got caught. They had to keep pryin' the fence up while I tried to untangle it. I was stuck for a while too. Even though I knew they wouldn't leave me, part of me was panicked enough to think they might not have any choice. The fence was very difficult to hold up—even for two people. Goodie and Chris couldn't hold it for long. They had to take breaks and then try again. The whole ordeal was a bit unnerving to say the least."

"It doesn't necessarily have to be a two-man job. I suppose someone could figure out another way," Porter said.

"No way! That fence was built solid, especially at the top where all the barbed wire is. Anyway, after a lot of swearin' and sweatin', they finally got me out."

"Yeah. I seem to remember Nick was awfully happy when he finally made it under the fence and back onto the legal side with me," Charles said. "I also remember all of us beginning to feel a little edgy. 'The Legend of Shoonuckha,' the birds flying up in the air, and then Nick's shirt gettin' caught; everybody was more than a little nervous at that point.

"Then as we tried to calm ourselves by watchin' for shooting stars, Goodie said he spotted a gopher, of all things. While lookin' up at the sky, I had no idea what he was talkin' about. Then he said, 'No, not up there, over there.' He pointed along the side of the hill on the illegal side of the fence, up by the water where we just were. We all looked. It was difficult to make out the figure. Our vision was aided only by the moonlight.

"We all stood up and stared over the side of the hill. Nick thought it was a squirrel. Chris said it might be a cat. I still couldn't figure out what in the world they all were talkin' about. Suddenly, I noticed a small silhouette of what looked like a head comin' toward us on the ground. It stood out against the light of the sky, reflected from the town below."

"I was convinced it was a gopher," Goodie said.

Nick jumped in, "When we all looked at it, it was about fifty yards away and up behind us on the illegal side of the fence where we just were."

Goodie continued, "So as this thing was creepin' toward us, we started playin' a guessing game as to what it was. At a distance it looked like a gopher, then a squirrel, then a cat or a dog. One thing we all agreed on was that it was gettin' closer and lookin' bigger and bigger."

I loved the way the guys were helping me tell the story because their first-hand accounts made it very realistic, but I wanted to finish it out for Julia all by myself so I took over once again. "It's important to point out that at no time did it make a sound and all we could make out was a tiny bump that stuck up off the side of the hill which we assumed was a head.

"It was thirty feet away then twenty...ten...five and then it did somethin' that puzzled us. It climbed all the way up to the top and planted itself there. Now all we could see was the top of the hill against the lighted background of the sky with a tiny bump stickin' up in the middle. It was directly behind us. We still couldn't figure out what it was, but there was one thing we knew for sure...it was starin' at us. It was listenin' to our guessing game. It was figurin' us out," I said, wide-eyed.

"Oh, God. I don't know if I wanna hear anymore," Kimmie said.

"It's okay. We're comin' to the end," Charles said. Yorkie and the gang pulled their chairs up even closer. Julia never said a word. She just stared at me from the other end of the table.

"Then Nick and I did somethin' very foolish. We walked up to the fence to get a closer look," I said.

"You didn't," Sam said.

"Yeah, can you believe it? I was tryin' to get these guys to follow me home, but they were determined to find out what it was," Charles said.

I continued, "I shook the fence to see if I could startle it so we could get a better look at what it was or maybe hear it make a sound. Nick and I were about ten feet below it when it did somethin' that made us think twice about gettin' so close. It started to get up almost as if it were stretchin' and we got a good idea as to the size of it.

"We saw the trunk of an animal that wasn't the size of a cat or a dog. It was the size of a leopard or a cheetah or some other jungle animal, we didn't know what it was, but it was big, much bigger than we thought! I remember shoutin', 'It's comin' right at us!' and then we turned and ran down that hill and out to the street so fast even you couldn't have caught us, Sam." He smiled.

"When we got to the street, we turned around to look for it. It was gone. Then it slowly and quietly reappeared by crawling back up to the top of the hill and planting itself. Once again all we could see was its head. Now it had a different point of view. We were right out in the open, standin' under a streetlight and it was starin' at us. We didn't know what this thing was, but it knew all about us. At that point, Nick and I thought we'd try to go back and throw a rock at it or somethin' stupid like that, but Charles dissuaded us," I said and looked at him.

"Yeah, I remember sayin' it could be a panther that escaped from the zoo and any second it could jump over the fence and have your entire head in its mouth before you knew what hit ya." Everyone laughed.

I smiled at my stupidity. "You were right. Well, it worked because we all decided it was time to go home. As we turned to walk away I stopped and said to the gang, 'We gotta take one last look before we go.' Everyone turned in unison. Then our biggest fears were recognized. It jumped up and stood facin' us as if it were staring us down. We witnessed...with our own eyes...the perfect silhouette...of a man. That's right, it was a human being. He turned to his side and ran, lightning speed, along the top of the hill. At this point, Goodie succinctly stated..." I pointed at him.

"Holy Shit! That's what I said." Everyone exploded in laughter. "Pardon my language, ladies. Finish the story, Chris."

"We watched him run along the top until he made it to the far end and then he disappeared. We ran all the way home and we haven't been back since," I said, relinquishing everyone's attention.

"That's one amazing story," Michael said, smiling at Sam.

"That was Shoonuckha, man. It had to be," Sam said.

Nick joined in again, "What really freaked me out was afterward when I thought about my shirt gettin' stuck. What if he, whoever he was, showed up when you guys were tryin' to get me free and he grabbed me?"

"We would've let go," I said. Everyone laughed. "I still don't know how he got up there all alone. It took two of us to get the fence pulled up high enough so a third guy could crawl under."

"What about the fact that you goofs were all up there by the water making all kinds of noise? What if he heard you and then came up from behind and pushed you in? You see, that's why I stayed on the other side," Charles said.

"Gee, you know, we took an entire lap around the top of the rez. We must've walked right by him at one point, right Chris?" Goodie said.

"Yeah, we must've. My favorite part is the fact that he knew that we were confused and didn't know what he was and he just listened and stared at us without making a sound or moving an inch. We figured out later on that the entire thing happened right after midnight, which officially made it Friday the 13th!"

"Wow! That's incredible. You guys have the greatest stories I've ever heard. You have to come over and tell the rest of the family, Chris," Anna said.

"Maybe the guy was Jack!" Kimmie said.

"Are you kiddin'? My chicken brother would never be crawlin' on his belly up on top of that pitch-black hill."

"What d'ya think of that one, Yorkie?" Nick asked.

"I think you get what you deserve when you're up to no good. Well, folks, all the fun is gonna have to come to an end. It's closin' time. Let's go."

"I still say I heard that sound, you know, DAH…dah…dah…dah. DAH…dah…dah…dah… as we ran down the hill."

"That was probably just the sound of the turds runnin' down your leg, Goodie," Porter said as everyone gathered their things.

"This has been fun, guys. We'll have to do it again. Thanks for everything," Sam said as he helped Martha with her coat.

"Anytime, Sam. Hey, Michael, let us know when your next track meet is. We'll come cheer ya on, okay? And don't forget we're playin' the Bulldogs next week," Nick said.

"I'll be there."

As everyone pushed in their chairs I noticed there was only one person left seated at the table. It was Julia. She was sitting there, staring at me with a gigantic grin on her face. We made eye contact and I smiled back. What a night!

"Does everybody have a ride home?" Charles called out.

"Are you kiddin'? We're all plannin' on crammin' into your uncle's car again. Right, sports fans? Hey, Julia, why don't you join us, we'll see if we can set a new record? Let's see, how many do we have…Chris, Kimmie, Charles, Anna, Goodie, me, Porter… Where's Porter?"

"That's funny. He was just here a minute ago," Goodie said.

"I'll come along if you're sure you have enough room," Julia said.

"We'll make room," I said, staring into her beautiful, brown eyes. We all filed out of the restaurant just ahead of Yorkie locking it up. After holding the door for Kimmie, I gestured for Julia to go ahead of me. She smiled and walked by.

SIXTEEN

"The shifts of fortune test the reliability of friends."

CICERO

Charles took his dominant seat behind the wheel of my uncle's cool car. We dropped Kimmie off first. I waited until her parents opened the door because she was so scared from all the stories. She told me she had a terrific night and thanked me over and over again.

When I got back in the car, I turned around to peek at Julia and noticed her angelic smile beaming back at me. God, she was pretty. As Charles pulled into Julia's driveway I rehearsed a few lines in my head for when I walked her up to the door.

Charles said, "Julia, would you like me to walk you up to the..."

I cut him off. "I'll do it!" I had my door open and my feet on the asphalt instantly. I walked around and opened the car door for her and then walked her up toward the house.

"We got you home before curfew, didn't we?"

"Oh, yeah. I still have ten minutes to spare," she said.

"One time I heard you say your dad can be kinda strict so I wanted to make sure we didn't get you into any trouble." I took a deep breath. I felt like I could not get enough oxygen.

"That's very considerate of you. You're a very thoughtful person aren't you...Christopher Thomas?" She stopped walking and stared straight into my baby blues.

"I try. Did ya...have fun tonight?"

"Loads. I'm glad my friend, Michelle, talked me into going."

"Oh, yeah, Michelle. We have history class together. She's nice. She likes to joke around with Woodcock a lot. She sorta teases him all the time, but he never catches on. Like the time she kept complimentin' him for growin' that stupid moustache. It looked awful, but she kept tellin' him it made him look ten years younger."

"Yeah, she likes to do that. Later on she'll tell me how she made his day. She really is a very kind person. Besides, if it gives her a chuckle and him some confidence then there's no harm in it, right?"

The headlights of the car started to make me sweat. I felt like I was in a line-up at the thirty-fourth precinct. I decided to turn it into a spotlight instead. I took a deep breath. "Hey, Julia ...you're not seein' anyone right now, are you?" I did it!

"No...are you?"

"No," I quickly blurted out. After a moment of uncomfortable silence I asked her if I could call her some time. Without hesitation, she offered seven numbers that I immediately committed to memory.

"You don't need to write that down?" she asked.

"I got it all right here," I said, touching my temple with my index finger.

"Well, I've had a really great time. Your family and friends are a lot of fun."

"Yeah. They're the best. Hey, I'll call you sometime, okay?" I said as she opened the front door.

"I'd like that." And then she was gone. I felt like a champ. I knew she was definitely interested and I had her phone number to prove it. I shadow boxed in front of the headlights for a few seconds like the champion I was and then I strutted back to the car like John Wayne after he just gunned down an outlaw. I slowly opened the door and plopped myself down into the seat.

"Well...tell us what happened," Anna said. Goodie, Nick, and Charles were all staring at me.

"I got her phone number," I said.

"That's my boy!" Charles beamed.

"Good man. You closed that deal pretty fast!" Nick said.

"I guess that hat and apron at Yorkie's hide a lot, huh?" Anna said.

"Boy, she's terrific, isn't she? I never realized how beautiful Julia is," Goodie said. "So, what's her phone number?"

"Her phone number? Quick! Give me a pen!" I furiously rummaged through the glove compartment. Nick spotted one and pointed it out. I grabbed it and immediately scribed those seven digits down onto the palm of my hand.

"Hey, Nick, how'd ya get outta that grounding?" I asked.

"I didn't. I snuck outta the house. My parents think I'm in bed sleepin'."

"We don't want you to get into any trouble."

121

"Don't worry about me. They won't check on me until morning. I just have to make sure I sneak in quietly that's all."

"Well, I know my brother is floatin' somewhere on cloud nine right now, but did you guys realize we still got another hour before we need to be home?" Charles asked.

"What d'ya wanna do?" Anna asked, looking around for ideas.

"Well, we don't need anymore food," Goodie said as he put his hands over his stomach.

"You know all the cheerleaders and football players are over at Murphy's. Anybody wanna check it out?" Nick asked.

"Oh, I don't know..." Goodie said.

"Why not? I haven't seen Mary all night. She's bound to be there. Let's go! It'll be fun," Anna said as she tugged on Charles's arm.

"You up for it, Chris?" Charles asked.

"Sure. I don't care. There's no pressure on me—I found my girl already. Goodie, don't worry, you can hang with me."

We arrived just a short while later and parked down the street near a bunch of other cars. As we walked into Murphy's driveway it was completely calm and quiet. I never expected it to be a small, white, three-bedroom ranch with green shutters and all the lights out.

My sister loved going to Murphy's parties with all her close friends. Mary was a good kid even though Charles and I picked on her a lot. The fundamental difference between her and us was she always drank at those parties. She never did anything foolish, but she liked to get buzzed. Charles and I tried to stay away from it. He went to a lot of the big parties and even hung out with the same people as Mary, but he never felt like he needed to drink.

I had not faced too many situations where it was an issue. That night would be my first real test. If I had been there with Elizabeth, I am sure I would not have lasted long. But with Julia on my mind, I was not worried about impressing anyone. I hoped everyone would leave me alone and I could blend into the crowd.

Anxious to see his football buddies, Nick led the way. We walked around the back of the house to this door that led outside from the basement. Nick knocked three times. In a house that appeared to be empty, we suddenly saw dozens of eyeballs peeking out from behind the shades of the windows. This was it.

Goodie's sneakers rocked from side to side like a tennis player awaiting a powerful serve. People never understood why he wore clothes with cartoon characters on them or why he was still fascinated by kids' toys. Goodie never had to explain himself to me. We shared a childlike sensibility. I knew we would be safe if we stuck together, just like the old days.

Mary answered the door with a huge smile, "Hey, look who's here! Now it's a party! Come on in. I'm on door duty tonight." She was not feeling any pain.

Murphy greeted us. He was larger than life. The six foot, four inch center of the basketball team was a genuinely nice guy. He always treated me well in school. I knew it was out of respect for Charles and Mary. He pounced on us with a beer in one hand and a cigarette in the other. "Hey, gang! How's it goin'? Anna, looking beautiful as always. Hey, there's our big shot new quarterback, Nick 'Strong Arm!' Charles and Chris, don't worry about your sister, we're keepin' a close eye on her. She's a well-behaved young woman."

"It looks like we should have our sister keep a close eye on you," Charles said.

"By the way, this is our friend, Goodie," I said.

"Nice to meet you, Goodie." Then he went into his Ed Sullivan impersonation. "Yes, folks we have a very big show tonight, a very big 'shoe!' Now let me welcome you all to my humble abode. I'll give you the guided tour of the lineup of all-stars we have booked for this evening," he said as he put his arm around Anna, spilling a few ounces of beer on her shoulder.

"To the left we have a veteran performer in our show tonight...my record collection that people are thumbing through...all the greatest Rock 'N' Roll hits you can imagine...Presley, Holly, Berry, Jerry Lee—anyone and everyone."

"Music is very important to a good show. It looks like you're well-prepared," I said, trying to play along.

He echoed, "Music is very important to a good show. So, help yourselves to those and spin a few around the turntable. To the right we have some newcomers on the scene, showing off their stuff in what I like to call our 'tough guy corner.' This is where my wonderful jock friends are proving their manhood through the ageless art form of arm wrestling. Of course, you can see the only girls over there are the actual girlfriends of the gentlemen themselves who are competing. No one else seems to give a damn." I loved this guy. He was a character.

"Does that mean if I go over there I can date one of those hunks?" Anna asked.

"Oh, you'd never stoop so low, Madam. And last, but certainly not least, we have the star of our show...the liquor cabinet. Yes, that's right folks...the parents are gone and soon that'll be empty. This part of our show tonight features some of the finest names in Hollywood: Mr. Jim Beam, Miss Southern Comfort, Uncle Vodka and Aunt Gin. But don't let the big boys and girls distract you from our good old selection of beer. We have plenty of bottles and even glasses for you aristocrats."

"Thanks for the tour, Murphy. It looks like there's a lot to do," Charles said. I was grateful he cut him off because I was getting a little tired of his impression of Sullivan—especially since it was not as good as mine.

"What's behind that curtain? Why do people look like they're waitin' in line?" Goodie asked. We all put our heads down in embarrassment.

"Well, that my friend is for couples who wanna take an 'intermission' from the show, if you will," Murphy said. "So let me know if you need anything, okay? Enjoy yourselves!" he said in his regular voice again. "Hey...I'm the only one allowed to finish off bottles of whiskey in this house!" he yelled to the gang at the liquor cabinet as he marched over to join them.

"Sounds like a lot of fun! Mary, show me where the rest of the girls are," Anna shouted over the music.

"Sure. What are you guys gonna do?"

"I wanna introduce them to my teammates," Nick said.

"We'll catch up with you later, Sis. Behave yourself," Charles said.

Nick led us over to the football players who were arm wrestling. You could not help but bump into people while moving from one side of the room to the other. The room was filled with smoke. The music was so loud people had to shout to hear each other.

I suppose Goodie and I looked like kids lost at the zoo. We shook hands with Nick's teammates and watched a few wrestling matches. They seemed like nice guys, but between watching them show off for their girls and chug beer, we quickly lost interest.

While Nick and the team's running back explained some offensive patterns to Charles, I took Goodie over to look at the records with me. We made small talk with some people while exploring Murphy's collection. Nick felt comfortable with his football buddies while Mary and Anna hung out with the cheerleaders. Charles had classes with a lot of people, but Goodie and I felt out of place. Most of the people at the party were older than we were.

After finishing up with the records, Goodie and I started to talk about Julia and how wonderful she was. I kept asking him if he really thought she liked me. He said I had to be crazy not to see it. We agreed I should definitely call her the next day. We spent the next hour "people watching."

Goodie and I tried not to be judgmental, but there were so many phony people there it was difficult not to be. The wrestling boys eventually took off their shirts to show off their huge muscles. I must admit there was a part of me that was a little jealous. I was lucky that a muscular physique did not matter to girls like Julia.

Next, we observed how this group of guys was blatantly hitting on some girls and the girls were laughing at everything the guys said, even if it was not remotely funny. I asked Goodie if he saw any girls he wanted to talk to. He said there were a few pretty ones, but he would rather just hang with me and observe.

The final component of the party was noticing how everyone dealt with the alcohol. We counted how many times people talked about it. The guys bragged about how much they could drink seventeen times in ten minutes and the girls mentioned how drunk they were twenty-two times in ten minutes. Wow. These were the coolest people in school? I could not believe I was ever afraid of this situation. I had proven a lot to myself over the first few weeks of school. I began to realize I could hold my own with anyone in that room.

Charles kept an eye on us from over in the corner with Nick and his friends. Nick drank a few beers because his teammates would have beaten the crap out of him if he did not. Charles smoothly stood by without touching a single drop. No one made him feel uncomfortable about it. A lot of the respect for him transferred over to me. They asked me if I wanted a drink. I calmly declined the offer and that was the end of it. No one even offered anything to Goodie; they had him pegged the minute he walked through the door. The way I see it is if someone as talented and caring as Goodie was labeled a loser because he did not drink, I considered myself in good company.

It was closing in on our curfew so I signaled the others to get going. We made sure Mary had a sober friend who would drive her home. The party was beginning to die down so she and Anna started cleaning up and taking the trash upstairs. Nick took Charles outside to watch the guys compete at who could walk the farthest on their hands. As Goodie and I started to make our move, I suddenly noticed two ugly heads appear from behind the magic curtain. It was Elizabeth and Deke. My heart dropped.

"I guess they made up because they certainly did a lot more than just make out," Goodie said. I made a fake laugh and then looked for Charles. I wanted to leave and I wanted to leave immediately. I looked out the window into the backyard, but he was not there. I could not find him. I could not find Nick either. I panicked. Where did they go? Did they forget about Goodie and me and already drive home?

"Well, look what we have here...a couple of fairies watchin' all the cool people party. Have you two been takin' notes?" Deke said as he tucked in his shirt. Everyone was staring at us. It became terribly quiet all of a sudden. I tried to look unshaken and calm, but a bead of sweat ran down my left temple. Deke closed in on us. He sensed fear. Goodie did not move.

While brushing her hair, Elizabeth joined in the assault by pointing at Goodie. "Who let this loser in? If people like him start hangin' around us, our reputation will be shot." The crowd seemed to be listening. I knew I had to do something.

"Maybe the two of you want a little time alone together behind the curtain, huh?" Deke said. They all started laughing at us.

"I guess at least he's a step up from that ugly girl you brought to the dance," Elizabeth said. Everyone gasped at the low blow. I could not stand there and take this. I thought of all the poor kids Deke tormented throughout his childhood, all the houses he vandalized, and all the adults he intimidated. Physically, Deke had the advantage, but verbally, I knew I could take him. That was my specialty.

I gathered myself together for a moment and then I let them have it. "I guess you have a really short memory, Elizabeth. Maybe it's that dumb, blond thing, I don't know. Need I remind you in front of everyone here that *you* asked *me* to the dance tonight? And *I* turned *you* down. I took Kimmie instead of you because she is a kind, considerate, and fun girl whose company I enjoy. While you, on the other hand, are an arrogant, self-centered, snotty brat who deserves spending the evening with this piece of trash. And that's why I dumped you on your phony, fat ass." They were both taken aback as everyone turned their heads from me back to them, anticipating a comeback.

"What'd you say, you little punk?"

"I'm sorry, Deke, I'm obviously talkin' over your head." Then I said with mock intonation, "Do you know what a piece of trash is? You know how your hair is all greasy and your pits smell...all the time? That's a good sign that you're ready for the dump."

"Chris, why don't you get out a box of crayons and draw him a picture of his future home? See if he can recognize a jail cell," Goodie said and the inebriated crowd cackled.

"You see, everyone here knows the only reason why you're here is because of her. Otherwise, you'd be hangin' out at the junkyard with your loser friends arguin' over whose mom slept with the most guys in town," I said. Elizabeth stood there completely dazed and dizzy. Deke could not take it. He exploded.

"I'm gonna kill you!" He broke off the end of a beer bottle. The girls screamed. I stared into the face of the jagged edge. He screamed at Goodie, "Get outta here Mickey Mouse boy. This is between me and him!" He lunged forward and pushed Goodie out of the way. It was just Deke and me, one-on-one. Insults would no longer work. I was shocked he was gonna cut me with a bottle. I looked around in desperation.

I tried to stall him. "Is that any way to act in front of these nice ladies? You certainly won't qualify as a gentleman, Deke, if you continue behaving this way. Besides, do you call this a fair fight?"

"I don't care about fair. I wanna slice up that pretty-boy face of yours." His eyes were lost. He was drunk and out of control. I knew I was done. All I could do was try to get the bottle out of his hand and hope I would not get cut too badly.

Mary came running from out of nowhere and before Deke knew it, she jumped on his back screaming, "Stop it! Get away from my brother, you piece of shit! Leave him alone!" In the confusion, Goodie grabbed Deke's hand and forced the bottle out to the floor.

Deke reached over his head to get Mary off. She was pulling his hair and choking him around the neck. Murphy quickly jumped in and pried her off of him. By this time Nick and his buddies heard all the commotion and came flying in through the back door. They pinned Deke against the wall in no time. Charles ran up to me.

"What happened?"

"This animal tried to cut me with a broken bottle."

"Are you okay?"

"I'm fine. Mary? Mary? Are you all right?" I ran over to her.

She pulled away from Murphy and straightened her clothes and then said, "I'm fine. Nobody is gonna mess with my little brother. Elizabeth, why don't you get your sorry ass outta here and take that garbage with you?" Anna stood next to her as a show of support.

Murphy took control, "All right, everybody. Everything's okay. Gentlemen, could you please escort these two to the door? Thank you. Let's turn the music back on. Let's have a few more drinks. The night is still young. Mary? Anna? Charles?"

"No thanks, Murphy. We gotta get home," Charles said.

As he got dragged to the door, Deke shouted over his shoulder, "This isn't over, Chris! You'll see...you'll get yours. Nobody talks to Deke Marshall like that. Nobody!" One of the football players slammed the door behind him.

"Sorry, little brother. Nick and I were bettin' with these guys to see who could walk the farthest on their hands. The ground was too uneven in the backyard so we went out front. I never should've let you outta my sight."

"Don't worry about it. It wasn't your fault," I said.

"I feel terrible too, Chris. He never would've tried that if we were here," Nick said.

"Hey, Goodie and I took care of it. We didn't need you two wimps around," Mary said. "That was pretty quick thinkin' on your part, Goodie. Nice job."

"I just reacted. I'm glad it's all over."

"Me too. The only thing is, somethin' tells me it ain't over yet...not by a long shot," I said as Murphy closed the door behind us.

~ SEVENTEEN ~

"It is a funny thing about life; if you refuse to accept anything but the best, you very often get it."

W. SOMERSET MAUGHAM

One of the most memorable parts of Sunday mornings was when my father would stand in the doorway of our bedroom and say one simple word, "Doughnuts!" He got us doughnuts from Morey's every Sunday. Morey's was this cider mill up the road from our house. They sold homemade doughnuts and fresh cider. Our family, alone, kept them in business for years. We all decided early on that their best doughnut, without a doubt, was the headlight. My dad used to buy a dozen of them to help make getting up on Sunday morning a bit more tolerable.

Headlights were round doughnuts—always soft and fresh. When the doughnuts finished frying, centers were inserted into the hollow middle. This kept the edges fresh as well as the middle. Rich chocolate icing covered the top and a little castle of white cream stood in the center. They were incredible! We would down them two or three at a time with a glass of Byrne Dairy chocolate milk—the best around. That was all I needed to start the day.

After eating breakfast, it was off to church. I loved messing around with Charles during Mass. That is, until Mom threw us a dirty look. Charles was not in the mood that particular day because his girl, Carolyn, was there. He watched her every move. I kept telling him he should ask her out. Charles was really sensitive and private about those things; he did not want Mom and Dad watching him.

After Mass, Mom convinced Dad to stay and talk to some of their friends from the old neighborhood where Dad grew up on Onondaga Street. Charles, Mary, and I were talking to some friends we had in grade school when I noticed Carolyn was all alone, reading the postings on the bulletin board in the back of the church.

I pulled Charles away from the crowd. "Would you guys excuse us for a minute? Charles, look who's over by the bulletin board, all alone. Mom and Dad are busy talkin' to their friends over there and Mary is preoccupied with her friends way over there. Now's your chance. C'mon you gotta go talk to her."

"Ya think so?"

"Yeah. This is a one-in-a-million opportunity. Just introduce yourself and tell her how beautiful you think she is."

"What?"

"I'm just kiddin'. Would you just go over there and make some small talk?"

"Okay. Okay. Go see if you can stall Mom and Dad."

Charles slowly walked up to her as she was copying down some information from one of the fliers that was posted.

"Hi! Ya know I've seen you lots of times here in church, but I don't think we've ever met. My name's Charles Thomas," he said and offered his hand.

"I'm Carolyn Thomson."

"Nice to meet you."

"You too."

"That's my brother, Chris, and my sister, Mary, and those two people over there are my parents."

"Oh, yeah. I've seen your family here a lot. You come every week, right?"

"Every single week. My brother and I were tryin' to figure out where you went to school. You don't go to Wilson High, do you?"

"No, I go to school here at Holy Family. I've been here since I was in kindergarten; that's how I first started coming to this church. My parents are good friends with Father Kennedy."

"Father Kennedy is the best," he said.

"Yeah, he's terrific. I've never met a nicer person in my entire life." There was an awkward moment of silence.

"So...do ya like the school here at Holy Family?"

"It's okay, but the classes are really small and I don't get to meet many people. There are only about twenty students in my grade."

"That's it? And what grade is that?"

"Ninth."

"Oh...I'm in eleventh over at Wilson." I joined my parents and got Dad to tell a few stories about when he played basketball in high school. Charles knew he did not have much time left. He could not think of where to go next so he just aimed right for the

131

target. "So Carolyn, would ya mind if I called you some night so we could talk?" He felt like she took an eternity to answer.

"No. I wouldn't mind...that would be okay. I just can't get calls after nine. My father is kinda strict about that. Let's see, where can I find a pen?" she said, looking all around.

"You don't have to write it down. Just tell me. I'll remember it." He laughed in his head, thinking of me the night before. She told him the number and reminded him about her father's rule.

"Don't worry. I'll remember. Thanks a lot, Carolyn. I'll call you and maybe we could go get somethin' to eat or somethin'." He knew he had to get out before it was too late. "Maybe you can help me learn how to sing the *Ave Maria* for Mass."

"That might be a tad bit too high for you."

"Well, how 'bout *Swing Low, Sweet Chariot*," he said, using his best bass voice.

"We'll think of somethin'," she giggled.

"I'll talk to you later, okay?"

"Bye, bye." She continued leafing through the papers on the board. Charles walked over to me with a huge smile on his face. I knew he did well.

"Well, did you get her number?" I asked.

A panicked look came over his face. "Quick! Give me a pen!" Pandemonium ensued.

Back when school started up Charles got me a job at Columbus bakery. They had the greatest Italian bread in the world, and they also made pies. During the holidays, the line of customers would stretch around the block. Soon after I was hired, Charles was able to squeeze Drew in too. Our boss was really cool. His name was Benito. He came right off the boat from Italy. He did not watch us every minute like some bosses do. If the place was clean, he left us alone.

There was a huge storage room in the back where we found time to get lost. One of our favorite games was pretending we were NFL kickers and trying to kick rolls of paper towels into this storage loft up by the ceiling. Besides screwing around on breaks, we used to eye the women that stopped in. There was a bell that hung over one of the ovens and we played this game where whenever a good-looking girl walked by, one of us would ring the bell. It was more subtle than shouting, "Hey, everybody come look, there's a hot babe out here!"

One of the other workers was a kid named Leo. He was Charles's age and a real nice kid. We teased him by ringing the bell every time his girlfriend came to buy bread. The look on Leo's face was priceless when he would hear the bell ring and come running out only to find us all staring at his girlfriend. We used to tease him that it was a huge compliment. He said he would prefer it if we just left her out of the whole equation, but he was a good sport about it for the most part.

Although the food was amazing, we could not just eat whatever we wanted. Benito's rule was that we could only eat damaged food that could not be sold to the public. After telling Drew how delicious the blueberry pies smelled, he walked over to the pie racks and grabbed one. Without hesitation, he dropped his fist down into the middle of it and said, "I guess they can't sell this one. Grab a couple of forks and meet me in the back." Charles almost wet his pants when I told him that one.

We sat on top of a couple of boxes of packaged flour and cut up the pie between us.

"Man, this is good!" I mumbled through a mouthful of pie.

"The best, isn't it? Next time we'll have to drop one of those sweet potato pies."

"You said it. Hey, Drew, we never really talked about the dance. Did you have a good time with Kathy?"

"Oh, yeah. We always have lots of fun and then on Monday she treats me like I'm some stranger," he said and took another bite.

"What is the matter with that girl? I just don't get her."

"Yeah, I don't either. But do any of us really *get* any of these girls? You treat 'em well and they run all over you and then you see guys at school treat their women like crap and they put up with it for years." He had a point.

"Hey, did I tell ya about Julia from Yorkie's Place?"

"No. I saw you two dancin' together. What's the story?"

"We drove her home and I found out she doesn't have a boyfriend. I got her number. I'm gonna call her tonight."

"Wow. That's terrific. Ya know, I always thought she was real nice at Yorkie's, but I never really noticed her too much."

"Ya know, it's kinda cool bein' able to sit and talk like this." I wiped the corners of my mouth. "Why don't you get out there and find somebody besides that Kathy? You know you could do better than her."

"Yeah? I don't know. My mind is spinnin' in all different directions." He put his fork down and slowly raised his head from the plate until his eyes met mine. He just stared at me for a few seconds.

"What?" I asked, feeling like he had something important to say.

"Can you keep a secret?"

"Sure."

"Ya know the way my family is really religious and we have Father Kennedy over for dinner all the time? Part of me really wants to be like him. Nobody knows this...but for a few years now...I've been wonderin' if maybe I should become a priest. What d'ya think?"

I was taken off guard. I stumbled over my words trying to think of something to say. "I think...you're a devout Catholic, right? You're good at helpin' those who are less-fortunate. Look what you've done for Jack all these years," I joked, trying to stall so I could find the right words to say. Drew laughed.

I continued, "Seriously, I think you'd make a great priest. I can see you doin' that. You're great with people and you're close to the church. Hey, maybe you could marry me and Julia someday." I tried to make him feel more comfortable by joking around. "Of course, I'm sure Jack and Charles and I could give you some great laughs in the confessional. Remember you can't share what you hear with anybody."

"Don't worry, all your horrible deeds would be safe with me," he laughed. "Anyway, my parents really think the priesthood would be good for me and I know I'd make them proud if I joined."

"I think you'd handle all that just fine, but the 'Million-Dollar Question' is...can you forget about women like Kathy and her hourglass figure?"

"I don't know. That's definitely the 'Million-Dollar Question,' isn't it? But seriously, I'm tired of people only thinkin' of themselves all the time. We need to look out for each other more often, like you and Charles. You guys always put each other first.

134

That's the way it should be. People need to start realizin' that. There are a lot of poor people and children in this world who need our help. If we don't help them, who will? I wanna get out there and influence people to create change in a positive way. I love this community and I wanna help in some way." I never realized how deep Drew was. I had a newfound respect for him.

"I guess I just have to pray about it and God will give me the answer I'm lookin' for. Father Kennedy's favorite quote is, 'Prayer doesn't change things for you, it changes you for things.' I think he's right. Anyway, thanks for listenin', Chris. It means a lot to me. Ya know I've always considered you to be one of my best friends."

"Remember to tell God that when you become ordained. Seriously, Drew, I feel the same. You remind me of one of those great philosophers like Socrates or Plato. You got a big heart, my friend." We sat there in silence for a moment.

"Ya don't think we should hug or somethin', do ya?"

I paused and said, "Nah."

"Me neither." The pie was done and so was our break. Drew got me thinking about my own future. That talk sparked something in me that caused some very serious introspection. If "all the world's a stage" I needed to figure out what my role was and how to play it.

We picked up our mops and spent the next twenty minutes convincing each other the Yankees would definitely win the World Series that year. We knew we had the hitting, but our pitching was suspect.

After a while, I was sort of in my own world, mopping until I suddenly heard the bell ring. I quickly ran out to the front of the bakery to see what pretty girl was there. Sure enough, there was Leo's girlfriend leaning over the counter, grabbing a round loaf of Italian bread. I looked over at Drew. He smiled and said, "I don't know, Chris, it's the 'Million-Dollar Question,' isn't it?"

~ EIGHTEEN ~

"The future belongs to those who believe in the beauty of their dreams."

ELEANOR ROOSEVELT

The time had come to make the call to Julia. Of course, I had to rehearse what I was going to say about twenty times before I dialed the number. My voice squeaked when I asked to speak with Julia—damn puberty. Her mom was very nice and tried not to laugh. Once Julia got on the phone I started to relax. We talked about school and what it was like for her to work at Yorkie's Place. We did not talk for very long before her sister needed to use the phone. I asked Julia if she would like to go to dinner and a movie with me some night and she said she would love to. The only problem was she would not be free until Friday. I had to wait all week. At least it gave me something to look forward to.

The week was filled with its usual excitement. Porter got sent to the Principal's Office twice, once for tampering with chemicals in the lab and causing a small explosion, and once for calling Mr. Bulbsey a "fat, hairy baboon." Not only did Bulbsey not like being called fat, but he was also very sensitive about the fact that he was as hairy as a primate. He had one big eyebrow, hairy knuckles, hairy ears, hairy arms, and we could only imagine what he was hiding under his shirt.

After Nick wrote a letter of apology to Mr. Woodcock, he got back to practice with the football team. The coach hated to leave him out of the Homecoming Game, especially since we lost by ten points, but it was Old Man Crutcher who ordered him to sit out. Nick was a godsend to Wilson High. He could throw the ball forty yards with near-collegiate accuracy. He originally got the opportunity to play after the starting quarterback broke his leg.

Goodie won first prize in an art competition. He drew a pen-and-ink sketch of an old, abandoned barn down the street from us. It was quite clever. From a distance it looked like he drew it with complicated lines and shading. Up close you could see the entire image was composed of an intricate series of dots. As usual

I marveled at his talent and bought him a Marble Farms milkshake to celebrate.

We also celebrated the news we read in the paper that the police finally caught that crazy guy who escaped from the mental institution. They apprehended him only about five blocks from his dad's house. Kids all over the neighborhood breathed a sigh a relief.

One day after school I took some of my money I had been saving and went shopping with Jack for some new clothes for my big date with Julia. We had some good talks about music, movies, school, friends, and family. Everything went well until this stupid kid behind the counter said something derogatory about Anna. I knew we were in trouble when Jack's nostrils began to flare. He ripped the arm off of one of the mannequins and chased the kid all over the store with it. He never actually hit him, but he sure did scare the daylights out of him.

Charles and I spent some time working at the bakery with Drew. It helped move the week along. Of course, a bunch of us found at least a couple of nights a week to stop by our favorite street corner and see what Ms. Turner was up to. Porter convinced us we were like her bodyguards and we had to check up on her every single night to make sure she was okay.

I made it a point to go out of my way to see Julia during the day. She always gave me a big smile and a short, polite conversation. I was so excited to take her out. Looking forward to our big date carried me through the entire week. And I was not the only one with good news. Carolyn Thomson agreed to go to the movies Friday night with Charles. He and I decided not to make it a double date because we did not want to cramp each other's style. We did agree to meet later on at the movie house.

The only real bad news was Deke Marshall kept telling people he was gonna find a way to get back at me. I tried to ignore it, but it really bothered me. The only thing that calmed me down was knowing I had plenty of people I could count on, inside and outside the walls of Wilson High.

Friday finally came around. Julia only lived a few blocks away from the restaurant and the movie house so I walked over to pick her up. If we spent the date on foot we would not have to worry about getting a ride from anyone. It was about a half-hour walk to her house, but my adrenaline carried me. Charles and I spent an hour getting ready. We would have been done faster, but we had to put up with Mary and Dad pestering us the entire time.

I had my coolest outfit picked out, one that Jack helped me put together. I wore my blue jeans with a brand new white T shirt, and a black leather watch. It was very comfortable, but it was not dressy enough so I threw on a navy sweater vest Jack picked out. Of course, the final piece to complete the ensemble was my red, James Dean jacket. I was ready. I told Charles I would meet him at the movie house for the seven o'clock show.

I arrived at Julia's house at ten minutes to five, awfully nervous about meeting her parents. Both of them came straight from Italy. Her father worked at the factory in town and her mom was a seamstress. I knew they had to be nice people to raise a girl like Julia, but I worried they might be weird about me taking her out. Her mother offered me a drink and then some chocolates. She was very kind. Julia's father was the one I was really worried about. She told me over and over again how strict he was.

We sat in the parlor and talked for about a half hour. Julia's dad insisted on showing me pictures from his hometown in Italy. It was spelled G-i-o-i. I guess it is pronounced like the word "joy." Then he asked all kinds of questions about my family. Where did we live? Where did my parents come from? What did they do for a living? No stone was left unturned.

Then he said it was a pleasure meeting me and he would also like to meet my parents someday. Julia gave me a big smile. She went over all the plans we had for the evening with him. Then he nodded his head in approval and we all stood up from the table. He shook my hand and said, "Make sure you have her home by ten o'clock, young man." I promised I would. I knew not to disappoint him. After we finished our polite conversation, Julia and I went out the front door.

"That went well, don't ya think?"

"Sure. Don't worry, my dad is a Teddy Bear. He just wants you to know he calls all the shots, that's all."

"Now, I'm gonna take you to the best pizza place in the world."

"Yeah, I love Pavone's. We're goin' to the one down on Jackson Street, right? My father says it's almost as good as the pizza back in Italy. Believe me, that's quite a compliment comin' from him."

We sat in the big booth by the front window so I could show off my beautiful date to anyone who walked by. We ordered a few slices of cheese pizza, a couple of Cherry Cokes, and we split a cheese calzone. That was my usual order whenever Charles and I went there. Calzones are these incredible dough sandwiches filled with mozzarella and ricotta cheese. They are one of my favorite foods in the world. Julia giggled as I dissected everything about the food that made Pavone's the best restaurant in the world.

"Do you get paid to talk like that? You're a walking advertisement," she said.

"I just grew up on this pizza. It's always been a big part of my life. To me, Pavone's Pizza means good food, yes, but it also means lunches with my brother, Charles, after playing baseball all morning. It means Saturday nights with my friends. It means a break between shoppin' with my parents and sister, Mary. There are a lot of great memories here." I devoured my slice.

"I think it's great the way family is important to you. It is to me too. You didn't get to meet my sister tonight. She was out with my cousin, but she and I have a relationship like you and Charles. We do everything together. We've shared a room since I was born." She took a sip of her drink.

"That's cool. Ya know, I think it's important. You learn a lot by sharin' a room. Charles and I have had some of the greatest conversations known to mankind during the wee hours of the morning in that little room of ours." She smiled and I could not help but think of how badly I wanted to kiss her. Her face was so bright and cheery. She made me feel so at ease. "I think that when I have kids, even if I have ten bedrooms in the house, I'll have 'em share."

"Really? That's interesting. So do you picture yourself having a large family?" she asked.

"Yeah...at least four or five kids. That's what makes a house a home, ya know?" I have to admit, I stopped for a moment and part of me hoped to God I had just given her the right answer. I did not want to scare her away on the first date.

"Wow! I guess your wife is gonna have to be quite a woman."

"Oh, yeah...of course, we'll have to make that decision together, right? After all, she'll be the one havin' 'em. How 'bout you? How many kids do you want? Three boys? Two girls?" I asked, trying to get the attention off of myself.

"Well, I think it's easier to only have two. I've always thought I'd definitely want at least two, but I think I'll decide after I have the first. Who knows, maybe after just one I'll see how hard it is and I won't wanna go through it again," she said.

"Well, you have plenty of time to think about it. Look at us, we're about ten years ahead of ourselves. Let's just worry about sharin' this last piece of pizza, okay?" We sat quietly for a moment and chewed our food. My mind raced to find the next topic we could discuss.

"Chris, does it bother you to talk about your future?"

"No, not at all. I just thought it sounded kinda funny for our first date. I'd be glad to talk about anything you want. I just didn't wanna make you uncomfortable, that's all."

"I'm not uncomfortable. My best friend, Michelle, and I talk about this stuff all the time. I think it's fun. Go ahead, ask me another question."

"Okay, well, what d'ya picture yourself doin' in ten years? You know, for a career?" I asked and then started in on the calzone.

"I don't know. My mother thinks I should be a teacher. I suppose I could. I've given it some thought. I can see myself working well with children and I like the whole school environment thing, I guess. My father says I have a good work ethic too and my friends tell me I'm a real people person. I've always thought teaching is an important job. So, maybe there's a future for me there."

I was fascinated by the way she ate. She never got a strand of cheese, a drop of sauce, or a crumb of crust on her face. She was so neat and clean.

"How 'bout you?"

I did not want to talk about me. I was too busy staring at her. "My dad's been in sales for years. I could probably take over his business when he retires. My sister, Mary, always tells me I should become a doctor 'cause I'll make a lot of money, but Charles thinks I could be a lawyer 'cause I'm such a good talker. I really don't know. I guess I'll just try to get good grades for now and figure it out later," I said and then I slurped down my Cherry Coke.

That was the best answer I could come up with. I really did not know for sure. This one was too hard to deal with. I suppose a girl as focused about life as Julia Romano had it all figured out, but I was different. I was just going to have to decide along the way.

She suddenly set her drink down on the table and looked up at me with this excited expression. "Ya know what I could see you doin'? I could see you bein' an actor or a writer or somethin'. You're a great storyteller and you do those impressions too. You put on quite a show at Yorkie's the other night."

"Me? Get outta here!"

"No, really, I mean it. The way you told that story the other night was amazing. Everyone's eyes were glued to you. You can hold an audience's attention better than anyone I know. You were so entertaining. You could definitely go far in something like that. You have so much energy and enthusiasm when you tell a story. In fact, that's the kind of enthusiasm a teacher has to create with his students in the classroom. I bet you'd make a great teacher too."

"Ya really think so?" I thought it over for a moment. "I guess I could be a teacher. I could talk to the kids the way I talk to my friends. I'd much rather be James Dean or Marlon Brando, but hey, I've got time to decide. Thanks for the input. You're too kind," I said, staring into her eyes. I felt like the conversation led to a perfect opportunity to kiss her, but the setting was not right. We could not share our first kiss with some guy in the background yellin', "One large pepperoni comin' up!" I decided I might try later on at the movie house. If not, then maybe I would take a shot right before I brought her home.

Julia sat, nursing her drink for a few minutes after we finished our food. I knew we had to leave in a bit if we wanted to make it to the movie on time. "Before we go…see the young guy with the moustache behind the counter? His name is Massimo. You wanna talk about entertaining? Just watch him do his thing for a few minutes. He's a riot," I said, turning to focus my attention.

Massimo was cutting a pizza with one hand while raining cheese down on some dough with the other. We listened in. "May I help who's next, please? What can I getcha? Two cheese calzones? Side of sauce?" Then he yelled down the counter, "Hey,

Gianluca, two cheese calzones comin' up with an 'SOS.'" Then he bobbed and weaved past the other employees to get over to the soda fountain, "Somethin' to wash it down? Coca-Cola, comin' right up!" he shouted. Flipping a cup into his hand, he poured the drinks while pulling the calzones out of the hot oven. It was like watching DaVinci paint or Mozart compose.

Julia was clearly enjoying the spectacle. He effortlessly glided over to the register, "That'll be one George Washington and one George Junior please."

Julia looked at me, "A dollar twenty-five, right?"

"Now you're catchin' on. We may have to get you a job over here," I said. "Watch how polite he is. He goes way outta his way to make the customers happy."

"Do ya have any preference regardin' your change, Miss? Whatever I got is okay? Boy that's a beautiful blouse, Miss. Keep smilin' and have a good day!" It was quite a performance.

After about ten more minutes of watching all the magic, we left Pavone's and walked toward the movie house. Of course, I entertained Julia by impersonating Massimo all the way down the street. She laughed a lot and said I sounded just like him. He pronounced every syllable in every word just like the characters in *Guys and Dolls*. He was easy to imitate.

When we got to the movie house I showed Julia this cool trick Porter showed me when I was a kid. If you go down the back alley and kick the door in just the right spot, it opens. Then you can easily sneak into the show without having to pay. We did it for years. Unfortunately, Julia felt uncomfortable not paying. She said she did not think what I did was right. I was so embarrassed. In a weird way, she had suddenly become a conscience for me. I realized she was right. I guess when you are a little kid things like that are cool, but that night it just felt dishonest.

We met Charles and Carolyn fifteen minutes before the show started. The girls used the powder room while Charles and I went to buy some candy. I told him what Julia said about sneaking into the movies. He laughed and said he told Carolyn how he used to do that too and she frowned on it so badly that he did not even think of trying it.

We all took our seats and the lights went down. We saw a movie called *Vertigo*. It was Alfred Hitchcock's latest picture, starring Jimmy Stewart and Kim Novak. We loved it. It was suspenseful and dramatic. There was even some romance so Charles and I could cuddle up close to our dates. We knew from the "sneaking in the back door" incident that kissing during the movie would probably be out of the question.

Carolyn had the whole movie figured out in the first twenty minutes. I enjoyed being surprised in the end. Julia and I shared a Hershey bar while Charles and Carolyn munched on popcorn. When the movie ended, Charles drove all of us back to our house so Mom and Dad could meet the girls.

We made lots of conversation in the car. Charles and I took advantage by trying to make each other look good. I spent ten minutes bragging about him and he spent ten minutes bragging about me. It was a remarkable evening. I was proud to experience it with my brother at my side.

Julia let me hold her hand a couple of times throughout the night. It was a gesture that sounds so simple, but it meant so much. I loved being with her. She made me feel so good. I could not believe there was a time when I went crazy over a girl like Elizabeth Allen. She was a fraction of Julia. Julia was attractive, honest, kind, intelligent, and funny. She was everything I wanted in a girl. When I was a child, I used to pray to God, asking him to send me an angel. He took his time, but I knew that night he had answered my prayer.

NINETEEN

"The human race has one really effective weapon, and that is laughter."

MARK TWAIN

As we pulled into the driveway, we noticed Uncle Bobby was over with Aunt Doreen, Jack, and Anna. Charles and I were a bit nervous about bringing the girls into such a crowded room, but we had faith we could pull it off. They all made a big fuss when we walked through the door. Mary did the honors of introducing the girls to the family. Then we all gathered around the dining room table for Harrison's half-moon cookies with milk and coffee.

Mom and Dad asked the girls about their families and school and all that boring stuff and then Dad took center stage and shared some funny stories like only he could. He loved having a new audience. Storytelling is somewhat of a lost art form. My father has always been a great storyteller. I loved listening to him tell us about his early years growing up. I studied him. I closely followed the way he delivered jokes, the way he scared the skin off of us with his spooky stories, and the way he did different voices and hand gestures. I sat back and watched my teacher show everyone how it was done.

He started in, "I'll tell you one of the most important things in life is a strong marriage. My mother used to tell me, 'Marry a good wife, you'll have a good life.' You must have a supportive spouse and I'll tell you kids I've got one of the best. You should've seen how supportive my wonderful wife was like when...oh, I don't know...how 'bout the time I fell down the stairs?"

"Are you really gonna tell that one again?" Mom said, rolling her eyes.

"How'd ya fall down the stairs, Uncle Jer?"

"Well, Jack, it sorta went like this. One summer afternoon my wife decided she wanted to switch our room with the boys' room because she needed the closet space. We spent all day rearranging the bedrooms. Now, when I exited my old room, the bathroom was on the left. From the new room, the bathroom was on the right. So I got up in the middle of the night and reached out with my hand to push the door open. That's right, I tumbled headfirst down the stairs." Everyone laughed.

"I've never seen anything so foolish in my entire life," Mom said.

"I hit every single stair on the way down, I yelled out every word in the book and I even created a few new ones. So what does my wife do when she turns the light on and sees the love of her life upside down on his back at the bottom of the stairs? She shouts down to me, 'You idiot, you just fell down the stairs!' And that, my friends, is the mark of a marriage made in heaven."

"I couldn't believe anyone could do something so stupid, that's all. I mean, don't you at least feel for the door before you throw your entire body into it?" Mom said.

"I agree with you, Pat. I can't imagine such a thing," Uncle Bobby said.

"Oh, yeah? Well, this is a good time to tell you kids the next most important thing in life is honesty. I seem to remember your Uncle Bobby learned this lesson the hard way." Dad looked over at his brother and smiled.

"No, Jerry, don't tell that one in front of my kids!" Uncle Bobby pleaded.

"Tell it, Uncle Jer! Tell it!" Anna shouted.

"One day your grandfather told Bobby here that if he caught him tellin' anymore lies he'd beat him within an inch of his life. Well, Bobby was out gettin' into trouble one night and the next day at the breakfast table your grandfather started to interrogate him. The conversation went like this, 'Son, what time did ya come in last night?' my father asked while reading his morning paper over his bowl of oatmeal.

"Bobby answered without looking up from his cereal, 'I came in around twelve o'clock.' Your grandpa said, 'That's funny because someone brought in the newspaper this mornin' and put it on the coffee table. I know they don't deliver it until at least five. Maybe I should call the police and tell them the paperboy broke into our house. What d'ya think?' He knew he had Bobby on the ropes.

"Then your grandpa asked, 'Who were ya out with last night?' Bobby hesitated for a moment and then answered, 'I was out with Terry.' Grandpa looked at him and said, 'That's funny. He called to see where ya were last night.' Bobby didn't move. He took a deep breath and said, 'Okay, Dad. I'm sorry. I didn't tell ya the truth. I was really out with Mickey.'

"Your grandpa folded up his newspaper and said, 'That's another funny coincidence because he called here to see where you were last night also.' Then he stood up from the table and said, 'Son, you have lied to me one time too many. Jerry, tell your mother to call the funeral director down the street. We may have some business for him. Bobby, go up to your room and wait for me,' he said and that was it. He never yelled or made a scene, but when your grandpa got upstairs, he made Bobby make some noises that only dogs could hear." We all laughed.

"I can still feel that belt on my behind," Uncle Bobby said.

"Yeah, Dad. You were so caught. That was the worst case of lyin' ever! I love it!" Jack said.

"Wait a minute here. This isn't the mouth of someone whose head got stuck between the bars of the railing on the front porch not once, not twice, but three times, is it?" Dad asked.

"What a loser!" Anna said. Julia and Carolyn enjoyed the familial banter.

"And is that the voice of the girl who stood up on the sailboat out on Oneida Lake and dumped her entire family into the water?" Dad said.

"Yeah. They told us all five times not to stand up. So what does my sister do? She stands up just as the wind picks up and flips the boat right over, knocking us all into the lake!" Jack said.

"Who's next, Mr. Thomas?" Julia asked.

"How 'bout Mary at the insurance office?" Mom said.

"What a beauty that was. I took Mary with me to fill out a claim at the insurance office. She couldn't have been any older than four or five. She never really even talked much up until that point. That winter our huge Weeping Willow tree fell down in our backyard. It took us a few weeks to cut it up and cart it off. I wanted to claim it on my insurance to get some money back to help me out. So I told the insurance agent the tree fell on my back porch and I needed money for repairs.

"All of a sudden, this one stands up and says, 'Daddy, that tree never landed on the house. It fell sideways, away from the house.' So I lost that argument. Then I told the agent I needed to be reimbursed for all the money I paid to have professionals cut up the tree and remove it. Once again this little face peeks over my shoulder and says, 'You and Uncle Bobby cut up that tree and hauled it away yourselves, remember?' I looked over at the agent and he said to me, 'Sir, next time you might wanna leave her home.'"

"That's priceless! And Jerry never brought her with him again," Uncle Bobby said.

"Do you have any stories about Charles?" Carolyn asked.

"Oh, yeah, Uncle Jer, tell 'em about the hand shake!" Anna said. Charles cringed in his seat.

"Well, my son, Charles here, decided when he was around fourteen years old that he needed a special handshake. It started out like a normal one, but then the palm came up around the other person's thumb. He thought it was really cool. He practiced it with his friends over and over. Charles became so used to doin' it, he almost didn't know any other way to shake a person's hand.

"Then Pat and I took him to orientation over at Wilson High. He was starting freshman year there in the fall. After the presentations, they gave a tour of the building. Then they devoted an hour to give families a chance to meet with the teachers. Well, on the way to meeting his teachers we ran into the principal, Mr. Crutcher.

"I stopped to introduce myself and my family and wouldn't you know it, when Charles went to shake his hand," Dad used Charles's hand to demonstrate, "he did step one and then went into step two and wrapped his palm around Mr. Crutcher's thumb." That line ignited the room in laughter. Carolyn would definitely be using that one on Charles down the road. Dad continued, "Crutcher handled it like a champ. He just ignored it. I couldn't believe my eyes. Seein' this old, stately gentleman give a 'hip' handshake without saying a word about it had us in stitches. We held it together until he left and then all three of us ran outside laughin'."

"I still don't know what possessed me to do that," Charles said.

"You must have some good ones about Chris," Julia said, hanging me out as bait.

"Do we ever!" Mary shouted. "Tell the one about the clown!"

"No, not the one about the clown!" I begged.

"My brilliant son decided he wanted to make some extra money a few summers ago so he decided to be a clown at children's parties. My wife was driving him to his first gig when a truck ran a red light and hit the car. Thank God, no one was hurt, but Chris was shaken up and upset because he needed to get to the gig and he didn't wanna be late.

"So picture this, he's standin' on the side of the road with his mother, rantin' and ravin' about how he was gonna be late. An angrier clown you've never seen. What really got him upset was when cars started honkin' their horns and wavin' at him as they passed. He didn't wanna wave. He didn't want to say hello. In fact, the only smile on his face was the one Mary painted on in red. The best part was that one family had the nerve to pull over and ask Chris to pose for a picture with their kids!" Julia was all red in the face and gasping for air, she laughed so hard.

"I'm sorry, Chris, but that's too funny!" she managed to get out.

"My favorite is the incident with the dog," Mom said.

"Oh please, not that one!" I said.

"I can't believe I almost forgot that one!" my Dad shouted. "We used to have a dog named Oscar. He was a mean, little daschund—ya know—a hot dog. Chris fought with him all the time. Well, one time Chris got too close when he was teasin' him and the dog bit him right in the face. Now, he wasn't bleedin' or anything, but his feelings were terribly hurt. Chris waited until no one was around and then he snuck up behind the dog and pushed him right down the stairs."

"I can't believe you'd do that!" Julia said.

"Julia, he was a mean, little son of a gun. He bit me in the face. Besides, I didn't hurt him that bad. He was tough."

"The climax of the whole story came later that night. We had company over and we were all gathered around the radio, listenin' to a scary episode of *Inner Sanctum*. Right in the middle of the program, Oscar walked over to Chris, who was lying on the rug in front of the radio, he lifted his leg, and peed all over him. I have never seen an animal act so human in all my life. Even the look on the dog's face showed contempt!" They were all cackling away while I sat there.

"Okay. Laugh at me all you want. That's all very funny. The dog peed on me, ha ha," I said. I had to put an end to the embarrassment. "Well, I think it's time to get Julia home before curfew. We must be goin'. Thanks for all the fun and humiliation." I knew my father had put on a great show, even if it was somewhat at my expense.

"Those are some great stories, Uncle Jer," Jack said.

"I need a tissue, my eyes are tearing up from laughin' so hard," Julia said.

Mom stood up and said, "Never a dull moment in this house, boy, I'll tell ya."

"Well, we all should be goin' now too. Thanks for the cookies and everything," Uncle Bobby said. My parents walked them out to their car and I told Julia I would like to walk her home if she did not mind. I wanted the night to last. Charles offered to give us a ride in Dad's car, but we had plenty of time to make it, so I wanted to walk. I needed some time alone with her. It was a clear night and I was hoping we could stop by the shrine on the way home. The shrine was a beautiful area behind Holy Family Church. I knew it would be kind of a romantic spot where I could ask her for a kiss. Besides, it could not hurt being close to the man upstairs when embarking on such an important mission.

~ TWENTY ~

"The thing always happens that you really believe in; and the belief in a thing makes it happen."

FRANK LLOYD WRIGHT

Unfortunately, Julia did not want to stop at the shrine on the way home. She said she was a little nervous about it getting dark out, but I thought she might have sensed what I had planned so she backed out. In retrospect, I understood where she was coming from. The first kiss is definitely something that cannot be rushed. I was disappointed, but overall I thought our date went very well. The movie was good, the food was great, and the conversation was memorable. She also seemed to feel very comfortable around my family. She laughed a lot at Dad's stories. That was a good sign.

I talked to Julia on the phone Saturday night, but I thought two dates in a row was asking too much. Instead, I let the weekend run its course and planned on seeing her again the following Saturday. It was difficult. When you are excited about something, a week can feel like a month. When I finally called to set the whole thing up I knew I could not wait until the evening to see her so I invited her over in the afternoon. I thought it would be a nice change of pace. She insisted on walking over to my house.

When I saw her come strolling up the driveway I was so anxious I could hardly breathe. She looked really cute in a pair of blue jeans and a red and white striped shirt. She was always such a well-put-together person. Her clothes, hair, make-up, jewelry—all flawless.

"How've you been? I feel like I haven't seen you in ages," I said as I opened the front gate for her. She gave me a warm hug. I thought I might have held on a little too long, but who could blame me.

"Yeah, I had a real busy week. I wasn't able to hang out around school for too long. I guess I was just overloaded with work. But I'm doing well. How 'bout you? Have you recovered from your family's 'tell-all' session last Friday?"

"Of course. We do that to each other all the time. I'm used to it by now. I hope they didn't ruin your opinion of me too much."

"Not at all. You're still that guy who did those great impressions and told all those incredible stories over at Yorkie's Place. I think your family's great too. I really enjoyed myself," she said as I walked her up the stairs to the front porch. I worried that there was a small part of her that did not trust me entirely because of my "sneaking into the movies" trick. I had to make up for it.

I wanted to be alone with her. I did not want anyone else telling stories about me either. My family was great, but they had been stealing the spotlight. It was my turn. I wanted to have her all to myself so I could show her the real me.

It had been a beautiful Saturday morning when I first woke up. The sun was shining, the birds were singing, and the neighbors were out working on their lawns. Then some dark clouds rolled in. It looked like a strong thunderstorm was about to douse the streets. I love when it rains. It is so relaxing and with Julia by my side it could certainly be romantic. I planned on us eating lunch out on the porch.

We lived in a home with a huge porch that swept around the front of the house all the way along the side. I thought it would be a good idea to sit over on the side where we could have some privacy. If we sat out front, my family could see us through the living room windows and the neighbors would talk. We were secluded on the side because there was just one small window from the kitchen. We would have a front-row seat when the rain began to fall. We sat down at my father's favorite table.

"This is a great porch! I feel so safe, tucked over here in this little nook," she said.

"Thanks, we like it. My mother likes to sit out in the front when my grandparents come over. They watch over everyone's business in the neighborhood. My dad usually reads the paper here in the morning. I like this spot the best because it is so private. Charles and I have had some important talks out here. Hey, would you like a glass of lemonade?"

"Sure. I'd love one." I fixed us two glasses of fresh lemonade and a plate of cheese and crackers to snack on. I gave myself a little pep talk in my mind while being harassed by my siblings. Mom fought them off for me.

By the time I made it back out to our little, romantic hideaway we had an addition to our private party. Nick was sitting in my seat at the table, talking to Julia. I quickly ran up to them.

"Hey, look who's here! It's our fearless quarterback. To what do we owe this honor?" I asked as I set the food down on the table. I had to search for a third chair to pull up to the table.

"Hey, sports fan. I was out doin' my afternoon jog when I saw Julia out here and I knew you must be close by so I thought I'd stop to see you guys."

I worked up a fake smile. "Great! Well, unfortunately, I only have two glasses of lemonade so you'll have to run home if you want one."

"Stop that, Chris. You know he's just teasin' right, Nick?"

"Oh, yeah, he's always got a funny joke to toss out."

"Tell us about your game and the interview! It must've been so exciting!" Julia said, bursting with energy. She turned her back to me and faced Nick. He went on for ten minutes about all the details of the game as he munched on the cheese and crackers. It seemed like ten hours.

Nick described how he had thrown three touchdowns and ran for one against Wilson's greatest rival, the Northside Bulldogs. He won the award for Onondaga County "Player of the Week." The newspaper interviewed him and everything. I could tell Julia was impressed. I loved this guy like he was a brother, but at that moment I wanted him to find the quickest way off of my porch. After five minutes or so I had lost all interest in his story and I started counting the beads of water running down the side of my glass.

Nick's voice slowly came back into my consciousness. "And that's when they said I won the award and the newspaper wanted an interview. I felt like Jim Brown or somethin'. It was incredible! The article is gonna run in next week's paper. My parents already bought a frame for it so they can hang it up in our living room. Coach Stewart said it was a great display of hard work and he thought I had a good chance of makin' the All-County team if I kept it up. It was great to have him go to bat for me like that, especially after gettin' benched last week. I guess I showed 'em, huh?"

"You sure did. Wow! What a story! You oughta be very proud of yourself," Julia said.

"Yeah, I only hope I can do just as well next weekend against Central. They have some really big linemen and they..."

I interrupted, "Yeah, you better be careful. Those boys don't mess around. One false move and your season could be over." I could not resist.

"Chris, c'mon now, don't say that. You'll be just fine, won't you, Nick?"

"Gee, I hope so." Suddenly I saw a head pop in from around the corner.

"Hey gang! How's it goin'?" Goodie said as he walked right up to Julia. He shook her hand. "Nice to see you again, Madam, gentlemen." Julia chuckled at the formality.

"Nice to see you too, Goodie. Pull up a chair!" she instructed him. We had a party on our hands. My luck was changing by the minute. It was going from bad to worse. The clouds started moving in around us. It was gonna rain all right. A rumble of thunder off in the distance made its presence known.

Julia leaped at Goodie with excitement. "You know what I wanted to ask you, Goodie? Is it true you worked with kids who are handicapped last summer?"

"Yeah. I had about three different kids I worked with down at Most Holy Rosary Church." He was very proud of the work he had done there. Unfortunately, I did not feel all that much pride at the moment.

"What was it like?" she asked.

"Well, it was challenging. I worked with this one eight-year-old kid who was paralyzed from the neck down. He sits in a wheelchair all day. His mind works well, but he can't move his body at all. At times he's able to move his head a little bit, but he doesn't talk much and when he tries to talk it's difficult to understand him. I was responsible for putting him on the bus and taking him off when we took the group on trips. I pushed him around in his wheelchair and had to feed him and change him—everything you can imagine."

"Wow, that's a great deal of responsibility," Julia said. I sat, stewing in the corner, eating the few crumbs that were left of the cheese and crackers.

"Yeah, it was, but I felt like it was important work. I knew the program needed someone persistent enough to move this kid around. Without me, he would have just sat at home all summer. It was up to me to help this kid have some fun, right? I was determined to go above and beyond what they asked of me."

I could not help but soften as I thought of Goodie wheeling this kid around town. I remembered that we did not see too much of him that summer because he was so busy.

"Tell 'em the good part, Goodie," Nick said.

This caught me by surprise. "What are ya talkin' about? What good part, Goodie? I don't remember a good part," I said.

"Well, at the end of the summer I planned a special tribute to my friend. I knew we had to finish the summer in style. This kid's mom told me he had always wanted to go on a roller coaster. She said it was the one thing he would probably never be able to do and it broke her heart. So, I made special arrangements with the bus driver to take us to Coney Island."

"You're kiddin'! You took a paralyzed kid to an amusement park? I don't believe it!" Julia said.

I joined in, "I didn't know ya did that, Goodie. That's remarkable!"

"Wait, it gets better. Tell 'em the best part of the story," Nick said.

"I took the kid for a ride on the roller coaster."

"No way!" Julia said.

"Yep. The guy who was runnin' it said he was a little nervous about doin' it, but I told him to strap him in just like everyone else. I said I'd sit next to him and hold onto him, so the guy finally agreed.

"When the coaster started climbin', this kid was laughin' and squealin' with excitement. You should've seen his face. I can't describe it. It had been a few years since his accident and I think for the first time since then, he felt normal. As the coaster plunged down the first drop he screamed with delight. I loved every minute of it."

"That's amazing. You made his dreams come true," Julia said.

"I can't believe I never heard that story! Hold on, I gotta get Charles out here." I ran inside to get my brother. I had not realized my cousin, Jack, had stopped by too. He and Charles were in the living room, listening to the ball game on the radio when I came running in. I invited them to join us on the porch and listen as Goodie performed a quick encore. Then the rain began to fall. Large strands of water pounded against the pavement. We all watched, quietly mesmerized by the dancing droplets.

Julia sat, looking pensive in the corner. "I think that's one of the greatest gifts I've ever heard a person give to another. Goodie, you gave that kid a second chance at life. You gave him an opportunity to soar in the sky."

"All right. I guess it's my turn now. Can I have the floor?" Jack said.

I interrupted, "Hold on, let me get a few more chairs so we can all sit down." We fixed our seats so we could see each other.

"You're not gonna do one of those splits or spins are ya?" Julia said, teasing him. "No. No. I too, have a story to tell," he said with mock formality. "This was back a few years ago, ya know, before I became a man. My father was out of town on business and my mom decided she would take Anna and me with her to go see our grandparents in Connecticut. My mom isn't a big fan of drivin' so we took the Greyhound bus.

"It wasn't all that bad, but there were some people who looked like they'd been ridin' for a long time, if you know what I mean. I passed the time on the way down by throwin' peanuts at this old guy's face while he slept. He was so stupid he never even caught on, but I digress.

"Anyway, on our way back home, the bus was very crowded when we got on. We couldn't find three seats near each other. After smackin' Anna in the back of the head, I ran to the rear of the bus and claimed my seat. Then my mom yelled at me and made me sit alone up front. The seat next to me was empty so I was a little nervous about who would take it."

Charles interrupted, "You? Nervous about sittin' next to a stranger? Nah!"

"All right, Mr. Sarcasm. So I'm sittin' in my seat and I'm watchin' out the window as this guy, about forty, hugs this old lady and then gets on the bus. Wouldn't ya know he walks right up to me and asks if he can take the window seat. He looked like a pretty harmless guy, kinda small and sorta Italian. We started movin' down the highway. After about a half an hour I looked over at him and I noticed he was cryin'."

"Oh, God, that's so sad," Julia said.

"Why d'ya think he was cryin'?" Goodie asked.

"Well, I sat quietly for about five minutes and then I finally decided I'd talk to him. Maybe I could get his mind off his troubles. So I started talkin' to him and I found out he was forced to leave his wife and kid because he had been struggling with alcoholism. His mother took him in for a while after he lost his job. The day we met he was on his way back home to his family and he was awfully nervous about it. He was a real nice guy. We talked about sports, he was a Pirates' fan, but I didn't hold that against him."

"If he knew what a Dodgers' fan you are, he wouldn't have admitted that," Charles said.

Jack smiled and then continued, "Before he knew it, his tears subsided. Then I told him about my family and school. A smile broke across his face as he reminisced with me about the good-old-days and how he met his wife. He actually was very interesting. It wasn't long before I had him laughin' and jokin' around with me.

"Before we came to the end of our ride, he decided to tell me the story about how he became an alcoholic and he lost his wife, his kid, his job, and basically his life, as he knew it. I think he just felt better sharing it with someone, ya know? We talked about how he could make up for all his mistakes by reconciling his wife and kid and tryin' to start over again. He seemed quite optimistic about the whole thing. It wasn't long before we got back into laughin' and jokin' around again. He had a great sense of humor.

"When the bus pulled into the depot he turned to me and said, 'Ya know what, Jack? You're a good kid. I'm glad I met you. You really pulled me out of my depression, at least, for a little while. I feel good about comin' back home—sorta like I'm a new man. I hope kids like you can learn from the mistakes of guys like me. Whatever you do...don't let anything come between you and your dreams.' Then he shook my hand. I turned to find my mother so I could introduce her to him, but when I turned back around he was gone. He vanished and I never saw him again, but I'll never forget the friend I made that day."

"That's touching, Jack," Julia said. He blushed.

"Ya never saw him again?" Nick asked.

"Nope. I've never seen him since, but we definitely affected each other. I mean, I helped him get over the heartache of being forced to leave his family and he gave me a few life lessons from all his experiences."

I stood up. "Well, I'm very impressed with all of you. This one with the player of the week interview...that one with the handicapped kid on the roller coaster...and now Jack playin' the 'Good Samaritan.' I never knew you guys had so much...integrity."

Julia turned and faced me. "You have some incredible friends here, Chris. You oughta be proud of 'em. Ya know there's an old sayin' that goes, 'People often judge you by the company you keep.' If that's the case, you must be pretty special yourself, Mr. Christopher Thomas." I never thought about it that way before. I felt so proud of these guys. I looked around and noticed the rain had tapered off and the sun started to peek out from behind the clouds.

"Well, this has been great, but I gotta get some stuff for my dad at the hardware store, so I better get goin'," Jack said as he stood up.

"Me too. I might as well finish my jog now that the rain has cleared. Hey, Charles, we're still on for basketball later, right?"

"Yep. I think Porter's comin' over too."

"This has been wonderful, gentlemen...oh...and lady. Hey, Chris, call me later, maybe we'll all catch a movie or somethin'," Goodie said as he put the chairs back in their original spots. Charles walked them all off of the porch and then went back into the house to listen to the end of the ball game.

Just at the point when I did not even want my friends around, they delivered these incredible displays of humanity and courage. Julia was right. They were exceptional people. I guess I never really took the time to notice it before.

Every word they said rang true in Julia's ears and helped her understand what we were all about. We were a group of guys who positively influenced each other just like Drew was saying that one day at work. They made me look good in front of Julia because they were such an integral part of my life. It was the greatest gift of friendship I could ever ask for.

Julia and I sat on the porch and reflected on everything we had heard. After some time, Mom invited her to stay for a steak dinner. She agreed. It was excellent. We took a long walk afterward and found ourselves down by the park. It was just about dusk. Being her usual carefree self, she suggested we play around on the swings. I was a little inhibited at first, but she pulled me out of it quickly. I could not believe she could get higher in the air than me. She was my own little angel. I knew I was falling in love for the first time.

The light was fading and I knew I had to get her home so we finished playing around and started to walk to her house. As we made our way up to the sidewalk I suddenly noticed a black '58 Dodge Royal pull up to the corner. It took a left and started heading in the opposite direction from us. Just when I thought we were in the clear, it turned around and very slowly started creeping up behind us.

I tried to convince myself Deke Marshall and his gang were not dumb enough to start trouble in the middle of town, but I knew I could not put anything past them. I grabbed Julia's hand and picked up the pace. As we walked faster, the car sped up.

"What's the hurry? My short legs can't move that fast," Julia said.

"I just wanna get you home before dark, that's all."

"We'll make it. There's at least ten more minutes of daylight." Ten more minutes was not enough. The sun that had broken through the clouds earlier was quickly falling and some of the streetlights had already come on. I cursed myself for not leaving the park sooner. They pulled up beside us. Without making eye contact, I noticed with my peripheral vision that the car was full of thugs. I spotted Benjamin, the paperboy, riding his bike on the other side of the street. I threw him a wave. He waved back and then took off down the street, pedaling as fast as he could.

The window in the backseat of the car slowly went down. I heard Deke's voice call out, "Hey, Thomas, pretty girl you got there. Is she available?" Julia squeezed my hand tightly.

I whispered to her, "Don't look at 'em and don't say a word. We gotta make it to the corner up by Yorkie's. Just keep walkin'." We were about two blocks away. There were houses to our left, but Marshall's car prevented us from getting to them. To our right was nothing but the open park, which the evening's darkness enveloped.

"What's the matter? Are you suddenly shy in front of company? You aren't so cocky now that your buddies ain't around. Hey, that reminds me, where's that cute sister of yours? My buddies and I were lookin' for her earlier. Man, I'd like to get to know her. We all would, right guys?"

I hated him with every fiber of my being, but I knew I could not say anything, otherwise, I might jeopardize Julia's safety. Once again I whispered to her, "Just keep walkin'. Don't worry. We'll be at Yorkie's soon and they won't try anything there." My parents always taught me to turn the other cheek, but if they came after Julia they would have to kill me because I would not let them touch her.

The car suddenly sped ahead of us and stopped abruptly. Julia jumped back. They all piled out of the car, kicking a few beer bottles out onto the road. We stopped walking. I froze.

"All right. Now let's settle this thing like men. You humiliated me, Thomas, in front of my girl so I think I should return the favor. That's fair, isn't it guys?" Deke slurred his words. The rest of the gang laughed and nodded in agreement. "The other thing is you tried to take Elizabeth away from me. In fact, she told me you even kissed her. So guess what? It's payback time. That sure is a cute girlie you have on your arm."

Julia hid behind me. I stood as tall as I could in front of her. I stared him down. "You'll have to get through me first, you son of a bitch."

"Who do you think you're talkin' to? I think you're gonna have to learn the hard way. All right, guys. Get him!" Four of his hoodlum buddies closed in on me. I threw some punches and even landed a few, but I could not hold them off. Julia frantically ran down the hill and into the park. Deke gave chase. I felt a punch to my jaw and then my arms pulled behind my back. My legs flew out from under me and my face hit the dirt. Blood sprayed from my chin.

As I lay down on the ground I could see Deke catch up with Julia and tackle her. I screamed for them to let me up. I could see her struggling and finally she landed her foot under his belt. He rolled over and collapsed onto his side. She immediately jumped up and ran deeper into the park.

"C'mon you guys. Get her!" Deke said, while gasping for air. His hands tucked between his legs as he lay in the fetal position. With a few kicks to the stomach, they knocked all the wind out of me. Leaving me on the ground in tremendous pain, they began their pursuit of Julia. Deke slowly arose and started after them. When I saw them gaining on her I got up with all my might, wiped the blood from my chin, and ran after them.

I could not see them as they disappeared into the darkness, but I heard them muffle Julia's scream and then one of them yelled, "Deke! We got her!" By the time I got down there, two of them were holding her against the backstop of the baseball diamond. Deke stood in front of her, drooling with revenge.

My face was warm and the open wound on my chin stung badly. Sharp pains shot through my abdomen. As I stood tall on the pitcher's mound I shouted, "Let her go! I swear to God I'll beat the hell outta every damn one of you!"

"Oh, look who's back," Deke said, turning around to face me. He pulled out his switchblade. The metal edge shone in the moonlight. "Let her go, boys." Julia ran over and wrapped her arms around me. I felt dizzy; my head was spinning.

"We don't really care about that bitch anyway. Do we boys? We wanna hurt you Thomas...real bad." They all circled around us. Julia crouched behind me for a moment and I felt her pick something up off of the ground. My vision was blurry. I could barely make out their figures. I kept trying to wake myself up from this awful nightmare. I saw the shiny instrument once again slowly waving back and forth in front of me.

It was the moment of truth. I could not let this monster beat me. I needed to prove I could stand up to anyone. I remember making out Deke's face for a split second as he said, "Your number is up, big shot!" As he lunged toward me, Julia took the rock she had concealed in her hand and threw it at him. It hit him square in the face, doubling him over. I felt my adrenaline burst as I kicked the knife out of his hand and tackled him down onto the ground. I jumped on his chest and punched him in the face with a left and then a right. His nose exploded. I could see my fists turn red as I pummeled him.

Then someone grabbed me from behind. It was the second-in-command. I jumped up and threw three ferocious punches at him. I connected with all three. I turned to see who was next. They all stood there dazed. I knew there were five guys, but I reacted like a caged animal, fighting for its freedom. When they saw what I had done to Deke and his partner they grabbed their injured buddies and headed back to their car. It was over. I collapsed next to Julia.

Off in the distance I heard some familiar voices come running down the hill and trade punches with Marshall's thugs before they could escape. The drunken fools were no match for Charles, Nick, and Porter. My boys beat them up pretty badly by the time the cops arrived. The last thing I remember, I was on the ground staring up at the stars in the sky. My friends were all gathered around me. I heard a crowd of people coming to see what all the commotion was.

"Chris...Chris, you okay?" Charles said, shaking me a few times. Julia was crying badly as she came down from the frightening ordeal.

"Little Benjamin came to us and said he thought old Marshall was gonna start trouble with you two. We got here as soon as we could," Nick said.

"Where's Julia? Is she okay?" I mumbled.

"Yeah and we got Marshall and all the rest of the guys. The cops just showed up. Can ya walk?" Porter asked.

I remember Charles shouting in a panic, "Someone get an ambulance...get an ambulance...an ambulance!" The faces blurred into the night.

~ TWENTY-ONE ~

"You will find as you look back upon your life that the moments when you have truly lived are the moments when you have done things in the spirit of love."

HENRY DRUMMOND

I woke up in a hospital bed with Mom and Dad standing over me. They told me I had, not one, but two broken ribs, twenty stitches in my chin, and a serious concussion that left me out cold for quite a while. The entire Marshall Gang was arrested and Julia was with her parents, explaining everything to the police.

I remember wanting to open doors for her, wanting to take care of her. As I lay in that bed I felt guilty about getting her involved in such a mess. Charles convinced me that it was not my fault. Mary said all the kids in the neighborhood thought I was a hero. That did not matter to me anymore. All I wanted was to see Julia and make sure she was okay.

The entire event was something of a blur to me. I remember my parents had a long talk with Mr. and Mrs. Romano. Julia's dad was very upset. He was convinced I was up to no good and selfishly put his daughter's life in jeopardy. My parents got most of the scoop from Charles and Mary. They covered everything that happened with Elizabeth, the dance, and the incident at Murphy's party. Then they explained it all to Julia's parents and they were able to iron the whole thing out.

Julia showed up with her parents for a visit on the morning I was discharged from the hospital. They were very polite and sensitive to my injuries. Julia's father even took a moment to thank me for risking my life to keep his daughter safe from harm. He became very emotional. I knew I had gained his respect.

My stay in the hospital was not all that bad. I had plenty of company. Besides my immediate family, who visited every day, Jack, Drew, and Anna brought me food and magazines. Nick carted in the first string of the football team so they could see an example of "true courage." Porter even stopped by to give me updates on the Yankees and Goodie showed up every single night to keep me company until visiting hours ended. He also drew me this great picture.

He made an eleven by fourteen pencil drawing of the gang. We were all dressed to the nines in suits and ties. When I told him I did not remember a time when all of us were dressed up like that, he explained that was because it was a picture that existed only in his mind. He pieced it together from different photographs and used his imagination to make it look authentic. He described how difficult it was imagining Porter in a suit and tie. Everyone was astounded by it. There we were—me, Charles, Nick, Goodie, Porter, Jack, and Drew. What a crew!

After a couple of days in the hospital, I was almost back to normal. I had missed quite a bit of school, but tons of my classmates said they would help me get caught up. People I barely knew went out of their way for me. Many of my teachers sent cards. Ms. Button and Mr. Dwyer even came to visit. They cheered me up one afternoon by sitting and laughing at all my impressions of the teachers at Wilson High. I will never forgot their kindness. They all gave me quite a warm welcome when I returned to school.

There were many other people who came to visit me also. My boss, Benito, delivered a fresh blueberry pie right from the bakery. Kimmie bought me flowers, and Michael and Sam stopped by with their girls and a box of chocolate fudge—my favorite. I could not believe all the love and support that came pouring out to me. I began to realize how blessed I was. I no longer needed to worry about feeling cool anymore. I was living a wonderful life and it was about time I realized it.

Throughout my recovery, Julia and I kept in close contact, but I did not want to pressure her into dating again too soon. Just as I needed time to heal physically, she needed time to recover emotionally. Toward the end of the first semester of school we made another date to see each other. I asked her to meet me at the shrine behind Holy Family Church.

The shrine is a beautiful, secluded spot where people go to pray or just be alone with their thoughts. Timeless statues and rainbow mosaics stood at the top of a hill inside an enormous dome of granite. In front of this awesome sight was an altar with rows of pews—all made of stone. When the weather was nice in the summer, Father Kennedy said Mass out there. Even though I was far away from everyone and everything up there, I never felt alone.

"Hey there, young fella." I heard a voice say from behind me. It was Father Kennedy.

"Hi, Father. How are ya?"

"Not too bad, Christopher. It's good to see you up and about again." He crossed over to me as I sat in the first pew.

"Yeah, I got into a little bit of trouble, but I'm better now," I confessed.

"That's good. I had a nice, long talk with your mom when it all happened. You were in the hospital for longer than expected, huh? We prayed for you in church." He sat down next to me.

"Thank you, Father. I appreciate that." At that moment a student from the school spotted Father Kennedy and approached him, asking if he would like to buy a chocolate bar to support the school band. After talking with the boy about music and discovering that he played the trumpet, Father asked him if he got to eat any of the chocolate himself.

"No, I don't have money to spend on chocolate," the boy said.

"Well, I'll tell ya what...here's a dime. Give me one chocolate bar, please." The boy put the coin in an envelope and then handed over the bar.

"Ya know what? I just remembered I'm not supposed to eat chocolate. At my age, it bothers my stomach somethin' terrible. Well, I've already bought it, now what am I gonna do? Say, do you happen to like chocolate?" he asked the young boy who panted like a begging dog. "Enjoy, Son" he said, handing the boy the bar and patting him on the head. Those were the kind of things Father Kennedy did all the time.

"Well, I'll tell ya somethin', Christopher. I sure am glad you only walked away with a couple of broken bones and some stitches. It could've been a lot worse."

"I know, Father. I suppose someone was watchin' over me, ya know? I'll tell ya one thing, the whole ordeal has made me appreciate my family and friends a lot more than I used to. It was incredible how many people were worried about me."

"Yep. It's a good thing you've come to realize that. Too many people never truly appreciate the life God has given them.

Unfortunately, it often takes some kind of tragedy to remind us of all we have.

"You know my mother used to always say to me, 'Ronald, you've got your whole life ahead of you. Don't dwell on the past, make the most of the present, and you'll build yourself a promising future.' I suppose that's the best advice I can give you right now. Take advantage of all the talents and abilities God has given you. Remember all those people who cared for you when you were down did so because every day of your life you've added something to theirs. You've enriched their lives as they've enriched yours. That's why they chose to give back to you.

"I'll tell ya, many people in this town would be a lot worse off if they didn't have you around—your family, friends, and schoolmates. I expect to see great things from you down the road, Mr. Thomas. Don't let me down. Be good," he said and then gently patted me on the head, stood up, and walked away. I watched him in silence and I felt renewed by a soothing breeze that passed over the hill.

I thought of the time when I dropped all my papers on the first day of school. I was such a frightened kid. I felt like I had aged years since then. I could still hear Ms. Button's voice say, 'Welcome to high school, Christopher Thomas. I hope you make the most of it.' I knew I was going to do just that.

Suddenly I heard a gentle voice call out, "Chris, have you been waiting here long?" I turned and saw Julia walking up the hill.

"No, I got here early. I like to sit and enjoy the quiet. You look great! How've ya been?" I asked as I walked over to her and gave her a big hug.

"Better, much better. I've missed you."

"I've missed you too." I stared into her eyes. "Come sit down. I have a lot to say to you and I even have a surprise too," I said. I took her by the hand and led her up to the first pew in front of the shrine. She sat down next to me.

I did not know exactly where to start. "I've been thinkin' a lot about you."

"I've been thinkin' a lot about you too."

"I don't know how to say this, but I'll try." At that moment I looked over her shoulder. Off into the distance I saw the tree way up on the edge of Bailey Hill. I never realized how visible it was from the shrine. I remember feeling so frightened when Nick flew out over the town. I could not push myself to do it. It was time for me to start taking chances. Father Kennedy's advice echoed in my mind.

I stared into her deep-brown eyes and spoke from my heart. "For the past few weeks, we haven't really seen each other at all and I've been miserable without you. When I spent that time in the hospital it made me think—I mean, really think about everything. I've finally realized what a lucky guy I am. I've come to treasure all that my family and friends mean to me. I feel like someone is tryin' to tell me somethin'. I think this has been a wake-up call for me. I'm gonna try to make the most of every single day of my life. I'm gonna use my talents to go after my dreams and I truly think I can do great things in this world. There's no more room for feeling all self-conscious or being full of self-doubt." I paused.

"That sounds great, Chris. I'm very happy for you," she said and looked down at the ground.

"But, I've also come to realize that none of that matters to me if I can't be with you." Her eyes lit up.

"You mean it, Chris?"

"You know I do," I said. She buried her head in my chest and nearly squeezed the life out of me. I held her close. I thought about how long I had dreamed of holding her like that.

"Now, I have somethin' I wanna give ya," I said and reached into my pocket.

"You bought me a gift?"

"It's not just any gift. This has been a tradition in my mother's family for generations now." I pulled out a gold ring and showed it to her.

"It's beautiful, Chris. I've never seen anything like it."

"It's a special ring that's part of my Irish Heritage. You see, the hands on either side represent our friendship, the crown at the top signifies our loyalty, and the heart in the middle symbolizes our love for one another. If you wear it with the heart pointing in it means your heart belongs to someone special." She was silent. I did not know what to think. "Julia? Julia, what's wrong? You don't like it?" She was crying. "Did I move too fast?"

166

"No...I love it," she said as she raised her head. I wiped a teardrop off of her cheek and gently pulled her toward me. We shared our first kiss. It was perfect.

"Can I put it on your finger?" I asked.

"I'd be honored if you would." I put the ring on her finger with the heart pointing in and she hugged me again. "You mean the world to me, Chris. I hope you know that."

"Remember that no matter what comes our way, we are bound together through friendship, loyalty, and love." The sun shone brightly behind the tallest tree on top of Bailey Hill as I felt my soul swing out over the edge and soar into the open space beyond.

Chris Merante has been a successful high school English teacher in the Greece Central School District for over twenty years. In that time, he has earned awards and praise from his colleagues and students. His efforts were recognized in 2008 when students voted for Chris to be the keynote speaker at commencement. The ceremony was held at the historic Eastman Theater in front of an audience of three thousand people. Chris shared his views on life with the graduates by using humor and humility.

Throughout his career, Chris has taught Creative Writing, Media Literacy, American Literature, British Literature, College Writing, Shakespeare, Drama, Poetry, Reading Remediation, and Film Appreciation at various grade levels. He also currently serves as a contributing writer and editorial director of St. Patrick's Magazine, a church publication that is the only one if its kind in New York State. Chris earned his Bachelor's Degree in Secondary English Education while graduating Magna Cum Laude from LeMoyne College in Syracuse, New York. He also earned a Master's Degree in Literacy while graduating with honors from Nazareth College in Rochester, New York. Chris currently lives in Upstate New York with his wife, Rita, their sons, Nicholas and Andrew, and twin daughters, Anna and Lana. For more information, check out Chris's website at chrismerante.com.